Inside Man

ALSO BY K. J. PARKER

INSIDE
MAN

K. J. PARKER

A TOM DOHERTY ASSOCIATES BOOK

NEW YORK

INSIDE MAN

Copyright © 2021 by Tom Holt

Cover art by Sam Weber
Cover design by Christine Foltzer

Edited by Jonathan Strahan

A Tordotcom Book
Published by Tom Doherty Associates
120 Broadway
New York, NY 10271

www.tor.com

Tor® is a registered trademark of
Macmillan Publishing Group, LLC.

ISBN 978-1-250-78615-9 (ebook)
ISBN 978-1-250-78614-2 (trade paperback)

First Edition: June 2021

Inside Man

BETTER THE DEVIL YOU KNOW, so allow me to introduce myself: I'm the Devil. Or at least, I'm his duly accredited proxy and representative, part of his organization, part of him in a deeply spiritual sense, flesh of his incorporeal flesh, spirit of his profoundly antisocial spirit. I do little jobs for him (actually, properly speaking, for *them*; he's a body corporate, like a swarm of flies—see under "My name is Legion: for we are many"), such as occasional tempting, a bit of general legwork, but mostly bread-and-butter demonic possession. In that capacity, I'm your worst nightmare, the most horrible thing that can possibly happen to you in this world or the next. You couldn't bear to look me in the face, something the sun and I have in common, but let's not go there quite yet. You really don't want me inside your head; trust me on this if on nothing else. It may therefore come as a bit of a surprise to you to learn that I'm basically on your side, or at least that we're ultimately singing from the same hymn sheet, you and I.

Suppose the hand dislikes the ear, and the ankle despises the shoulder blade, and the appendix thinks the colon is full of it. Would it matter, so long as they all obey the brain and believe in what it's trying to do? Maybe the rain hates the sea—I don't know. They all have something in common. We all do, even you and me. I like to think that what we have in common is what's right.

Other people, however, don't necessarily share our view.

~

My current assignment is about as far down the prestige list as you can get without dropping off the bottom of the page, but it suits me just fine. Actually, it's difficult, demanding work, calling for intelligence, patience, resourcefulness, and—how shall I put it?—a certain refinement and sensitivity that many of my colleagues, admirable officers in so many respects, lack.

I do liturgical compliance at the Third Horn monastery. Nice place; I like it there. I particularly love the west cloister. It's got an exquisite herb garden in the middle, with a small fountain that catches the midday sun. The chapel, which is bigger than most cathedrals, is early Reformed Mannerist, with a stunning rose window as you come in the south door and a forest of dead straight red marble pillars shooting up fifty feet and then blossoming into the most amazing traceries, like fingers spread to support a gossamer sky. Maybe the Brothers were a bit too lavish with the gold leaf here and there—in ecclesiastical interior design, there's a wafer-thin no-man's-land between pious zeal and vulgarity, but they neglected to tell the Mannerists that; the overall effect is nevertheless pleasing to the metaphorical eye and soothing to the nerves. In the Third Horn chapel, I feel at home. I feel *safe.*

Liturgical compliance monitoring—LitComMon as they call it at Divisional HQ, though I really wish they wouldn't—is more of an art than a skill, if you ask me. A thousand years ago, the Third Horn was endowed by Duke Sighvat III to sing masses for his soul in perpetuity, in shifts, round the clock; the idea being that if you can afford to pay Holy Mother Church a very large sum of money, then once you're dead, a continuous, unbroken chorus of prayer will rise up from the exceptionally pious monks of the Third Horn, imploring divine mercy for your soul for ever and ever. The logic is irresistible. No matter that when you were alive, you were as evil as a barrel full of rats and that you died in your sins, entirely unrepentant. The Third Horn monks, the very best saints that money can buy, are men of such irreproachable sanctity that He can deny them nothing; therefore, you are forgiven for their sakes, not your own. It's a sweet deal at a sensible price. Say I sent you.

Which is where I come in; that is, me or someone else

pulling light duty on account of fragility, incompetence, or being someone's metaphorical brother-in-law. The monks offer up prayers for the dead twenty-four seven, using precisely calculated forms of liturgy of known and proven effectiveness, the same formulae over and over again, like lawyers conveying a freehold, while unending ages run. My job is to sidle up to a choir monk in full flow; slip in through his ear, eye socket, or open mouth; and distract him, insinuating into his mind an irrelevant, mundane thought, sapping his concentration so that he mumbles, lets the stress fall on the wrong syllable, gets a word wrong or in the wrong order, maybe misses out a whole phrase. That, naturally, invalidates the whole prayer—those who live by the letter of the law die by the letter of the law, and you can't have it both ways—and the soul of some evil rich bastard has a nasty five minutes in the blissful Hereafter, until the next cycle of prayer starts and he's safely enveloped once again in protective intercession.

There's more to it, actually, than meets the metaphorical eye. The Third Horn boys are hardened professionals, carefully selected and highly trained. You can forget trying to interest them in images of naked women and wild debauchery, or anything so crude as that. Your rustic provincial monk can usually be distracted by resentful thoughts about his colleagues—*why does* he *always get to carry the thurible at vespers on the third Tuesday in Annun-*

ciation, it's so unfair—but try that on a Third Horner, and he'll laugh in your metaphorical face. The usual approach adopted by my colleagues, and standard operating procedure in the field operations manual, is to seek to undermine the citadel of faith with the saps and petards of doubt—as the Brother repeats the same mantra for the twentieth time that morning, you whisper in his ear, *What does this actually mean? Does it mean* anything? *Come on, admit it—you're wasting your time, and all of this is futile.*

We have our established procedures, time-honored and enshrined in the Book of Rules. They don't work, but we have them and we carry on trying them, because our orders tell us to. In my experience, doubt glides off the case-hardened faith of a Third Horn monk like water off oilcloth; one of us is wasting his time in a futile act of faith, but it's not the monk—it's me. So I have my own approach, which from time to time actually works. Normally wild horses wouldn't drag the secret out of me, but what the heck.

The way I do it is this: Forget the naked floozies, the resentful thoughts, the nagging doubts. You're playing to the other guy's strengths, and you'll lose. No, go for him where he's vulnerable. So, when he's locked in prayer, concentrating on his devotions with every fiber of his being, I offer him a fleeting glimpse of the transcendent. I share with him—just for a split second—my own memories of what it was like before the Unfortunate Event. For a fraction of a heartbeat, he stands where I once stood, bathed in the glorious light of the Word, on the right hand of the eternal throne, looking up into the face of the Everlasting and seeing reflected there—

Yes, I know. It's a rotten trick to play on anyone, let alone a holy man, but sometimes it works, and all's fair in good and evil. The better the monk, the more successful it's likely to be, and I maintain that everyone's a winner: he gets a moment of transcendent revelation, I get ten points for distracting his attention, the evil sinner in the Hereafter gets a timely reminder of what he paid all that money for—and what excellent value he usually gets for it, except when I happen to be on the job.

Well, not everyone. I get my ten points, but in order to share the memory, I have to reopen it. That's rather a high price to pay for ten points. So, some of the time I'm a conscientious officer and do my duty to the best of my ability, even though it's agonizingly painful, and some of the time I'm a conscientious officer and do my duty the way I'm supposed to, according to the procedure set out in the field operations manual, even though it doesn't work. I'm only obeying orders, after all.

So there we are, me and Brother Eusebius, who's basically all right in my book. He's seventy-six years old, joined the order as a novice when he was nine; as of compline today, he's recited the mass for the dead 142,773 times. There's a thing called muscle memory. It's how archers and swordsmen and athletes train. You do something often enough, your body can do it perfectly, even when your mind is miles away. The muscles that control Brother Eusebius's tongue and larynx run as smoothly and efficiently as the great mechanical clock in the Third Horn bell tower: word-perfect, unflappable, automatic. His mind is away with me, gazing into the ineffable light of His presence, but his lips are still shaping the magic words, in exactly the right order, with the stresses in exactly the right places. I enjoy a challenge, but this guy's got me beaten. Ah well. Tomorrow is another day, and tomorrow and tomorrow. No big deal. Light duty.

~

I'm on light duty because I'm officially fragile. That's the new buzzword at Division. It means you had a bad experience at some point that left you no bloody use to anybody. You spend a lot of time sitting in complete darkness, people have to repeat things several times before you reply, and unexpected loud noises or someone asking you to pass the mustard is likely to reduce you to floods of hysterical tears. Not your fault, you can't help it, your record shows that you were once a brave and reliable officer with a bright future ahead of you in Applied Evil, but that was then and this is now and we have a department to run. You're still on the books, and something has to be found for you to do. This theoretically counts as work, and if you fuck it up, nobody will know or care. Have at it, therefore. Cry "Havoc!" and let slip the squirrels of war.

Absolutely. I had a bad experience once. I prefer not to talk about it, if you don't mind.

~

Brother Eusebius comes off shift in the early hours of the morning and heads for the refectory, where I'm waiting for him with sesame-seed rolls and mulled wine. They believe in austerity at the Third Horn, in the same way that they believe in the Sashan Empire: it's real and it's in all the books, but nothing to do with us. A quarter to three, and no one in the place but him and me, definitely an opportunity worth following up. Brother Eusebius is a good man, but he has an inquiring mind, and what he's been seeing lately makes him wonder—

He sees me inside a deacon from Odryssa visiting the Third Horn library to consult a commentary on Theodosius. There's always one or two new faces in a big, cosmopolitan monastery like the Third Horn; it's one of the things he and I both like about the place. I happen to know, having been inside his mind earlier, that he's rather fond of sesame-seed rolls, which is why I crept into Brother Cellarer's head and planted there the notion of baking them today. Some people might call it demonic possession, but to me, it's just being considerate.

Brother Eusebius nibbles the end off his roll and looks at me over it. "Not bad."

"Personally," I reply, "I could do without the hint of cinnamon."

"Me, too, but nothing's ever perfect. Thank you."

Oh. "What for?"

He smiles at me. "Sometimes, to win us to our harm," he says with his mouth full, "the instruments of darkness bring us buns. Not that I'm complaining, mind you."

I think something uncouth, under my breath. "How did you know?"

"Oh, come on," he says, not unkindly. "I've been a monk here for sixty-seven years. I can spot one of your lot a mile off."

And that's me told. I sigh.

"Don't beat yourself up about it," he says. He's a short man with dark skin, white hair, and pale brown eyes. "Actually, you're not bad—you'd fool most of the pinheads we get in the profession these days." He nibbles a bit more of his bun. "Was that you inside my head earlier?"

I nod. "Sorry about that."

"No, please, don't apologize." He leans forward a little.

"I've got to ask. Was that—real?"

"Excuse me?"

"What you showed me." There's a certain urgency in his voice, just a faint pink tinge of blood in the water. "Was that—?"

"My memory," I say. "Yes. Unaltered and unredacted, for what it's worth."

"Really real?"

"Do you honestly think I could make something like that up? Besides, there's rules about that sort of thing."

"Rules? Honestly?"

"A code of conduct. So, yes, that's a genuine memory. From before the—"

"Yes, of course." He's anxious to spare me the embarrassment, bless him. "So there really is a—?"

"Yes."

"Ah." He looks at me, his eyes shining. "And He—?"

"Exists, yes." Pause. "I thought you knew that."

"Believed," he says softly. "As opposed to knowing. There's a difference."

"I suppose so," I say. "Well, then. And now you know."

"As opposed to believing." He frowns slightly. "Rather an extraordinary position to be in, for someone in my line of work. Being *sure,* I mean."

That makes me smile. "You've always believed, though."

"Oh, definitely." He's telling the truth. "Never a moment's doubt in seventy years."

"Does knowing—spoil it?"

"Not exactly," he says after a moment's thought. "It makes a difference, definitely."

"But in a good way."

"On balance, I think so, yes."

"Glad to have been able to help."

He looks at me. "Are you?"

I shrug. "He exists," I say. "Where I come from, that's not exactly a state secret. It's you people who make everything so complicated."

"Ah. Well, in that case, thank you."

"My pleasure. Sometimes one has to be kind to be cruel, after all." Pause. "I hesitate to mention it, but a small token in return—"

He looks up sharply. "I'm not sure about that."

"Oh, go on." My most charming smile. "It's not much to ask. A misplaced pronoun or a slurred consonant, that's all—just enough to make the blessed Sighvat choke on his sherbet. A momentary lapse in concentration, and next time after that, you do it perfectly. It's not going to kill anybody."

"Doing deals with the—"

"It's not a deal," I point out, "since you've already received the benefit, free, gratis, and for nothing. Therefore, there would be no—"

"Collusion?"

"I believe the correct legal jargon is *consideration*. No bargain. Just a graceful gesture of thanks on your part. Call it a professional courtesy, from one old lag to another."

"I don't know." He looks at me.

I sigh. "It's one of those cases," I say, "where the order of events is of the essence. If I came to you and said, 'Snafu the mass for the dead, and *in return* I'll show you the face of the living God,' then, yes, that would be actionable and we'd have you for it. But where there's no reciprocity, and no ongoing obligation—"

"Moral obligation."

"Moral obligation to one of our lot? Oh please."

He grins. "It would be a sin."

"True," I say. "But a forgivable one."

"If you do the sin with the intention of repenting later, the repentance doesn't count."

"Tell you what," I say, "I'll pray for you. How would that be?"

"Try one of these rolls," he says. "They're really very good."

If at first you don't succeed—"I met him," I say. "Once."

"Sorry, who?"

"Sighvat the Third," I tell him. "The evil little shit you spend your life praying for."

"Ah. Him."

"Yes. Would you like me to tell you about him? Some of the stuff he did?"

"Not particularly, no."

"I wouldn't say we were exactly close, Sighvat and me," I go on, "but I knew him quite well. Very well. Inside out, you might say."

"Ah."

"I was in his mind," I continue, though I don't like making Brother Eusebius feel uncomfortable. "Deep inside his head."

Eusebius nods slowly. "What was it like?"

"To coin a phrase, furnished accommodation. Everything I could possibly want was right there already, waiting for me."

"I see."

"And that's the man who," I say, "thanks to your ceaseless intercession, reclines at ease in the company of the blessed elect. Actually, I'm surprised he wants to. Fish out of water, if you follow me. He must get dreadfully lonely."

"They do say, hell for company." He frowns. "His money endowed the monastery, which for a thousand years has been feeding and clothing the hungry and homeless, educating the children of the poor, healing the sick, preserving the text of the scriptures—"

"'The evil that men do lives after them; the good is oft

interred with their bones.' Only arse about face, in this instance. Quite. It would only be a very brief interruption. No permanent harm done."

He looks me in the eye. I don't blink. "Not to him."

I sigh. "Fine," I say. "You win. Though in all fairness, I should point out that ingratitude is also a sin."

"Nobody's perfect." He grins. "I'll pray for you if you like."

"Thanks," I say, "but I have an idea I'm a bit above your prayer grade. No offense."

"None taken. And it's the thought that counts."

"No," I tell him. "It isn't."

No rest for the wicked, so I disembody and trudge back to the chapel to try my luck with Brother Hildebrand on the day shift. Hildebrand was a mercenary soldier for twenty-six years before he heard the call—faith like concrete but not the sharpest knife in the drawer, theologically speaking. Unfortunately—

"Hello," says my old comrade in arms. "What are you doing here?"

"Lofty?"

"Keep your voice down," Lofty hisses, loud enough to wake the quick and the dead. "He'll hear you."

Lofty's not his real name, of course. It's just a nickname, something I call him because it annoys him. Why he finds it so annoying, neither of us can remember. He's exactly the same age as me, to the nanosecond, and we've been getting on each other's nerves and under each other's feet for all Time.

"Sorry," I say. "I didn't realize."

"That's perfectly all right," Lofty says. "Not a problem. And if sixteen years of slow, patient work goes gurgling down the pipes just because you happen to come crashing in, shouting the odds at the top of your voice, so fucking what? I can always go back to square one and start over again."

I never liked him much, even before the Fall. I have a shrewd suspicion he doesn't like me either. "Has it really been sixteen years?" I ask him. "Good heavens. Seems like it was only yesterday—"

"Go away."

"My pleasure," I say truthfully.

~

Sixteen years, what we in the trade call a sleeper job. A speciality of mine, as it happens, before I got fragile. Typically, a sleeper is someone identified at a very early stage as being useful to the Plan. He might have certain qualities of mind, soul, or body, or a destiny that'll put him in exactly the right place at the right time.

I once spent eleven years in the mind of a poor widow

who sold cabbages out back of the Poverty & Justice, at the Hippodrome end of Brook Street, just before the war. She was nobody: nobody's wife, nobody's daughter, nobody's mother, nobody's reliable tenant or valued employee. Nobody would ever miss her, take any notice if she started acting funny—or funnier than she usually did, poor addled creature. Even if I got rumbled, nobody would pay good money to have her put right, because that's work for highly trained specialists, and their services are expensive. Seen as too ugly and too dumb to be worth exploiting. (I don't think I'd want to be a human, somehow; you people never seem to have got the knack of looking out for each other.) She wasn't worth anything to anybody, except me.

Eleven years, and she never once suspected I was there. But on a certain day in June AUC1171, she took a knife, hid it up her sleeve, joined the crowd outside the Golden Spire temple just as the Grand Duke was coming out after Mass, and stabbed him three times in the neck before anyone could stop her. Which she wouldn't have done if I hadn't been deep in her head all that time, twisting her mind and rubbing memories into her wounds, lovingly nurturing her resentments and warping her perspectives to the point where what she did was simply inevitable. And that, boys and girls, is what caused the First Social War (sixty million dead, if you add in the famine victims), proof if any were needed that sleepers really do work, and I don't give a damn what the bean counters at Division say about inappropriate use of resources.

The only thing I'd be inclined to question was assigning Lofty to sleeper duty. It calls for certain qualities, not least among them patience, resolve, a cool head, the ability to think on your feet—don't get me wrong, he's a good officer in his way. I know of nobody better at draining every last scrap and scruple of joy out of life, flooding minds with black despair, shattering faith, dispelling hope—good, basic, bread-and-butter stuff like that. But finesse? Do me a favor. The proverbial bull in a china shop. The sort who'd trip over something in the middle of the desert.

"Perfectly true," says Divisional Command when I raise the issue. "He's a clown. Solid marble from the neck up and two left feet. Trouble is, who else have we got right now?" He looks at me.

I look away.

(Did I mention the slight difference of opinion between Area and Division, on the subject of my fragility? Area maintains that I'm a basket case and should never work on anything Grade 3 or above ever again. Division takes the view that I used to be a basket case but I've had a long time to get better, and they're the ones who have to find the manpower for all the wizard schemes Area comes up with, and the talent pool isn't exactly infinite. I must confess, I'm with Area on this one. Of course, my feelings on the matter count for absolutely nothing at all.)

"Is this something I need to know about?" I ask.

"You? Heavens, no." He looks at me as though he's just bitten into an apple in a garden and found me there. "This is big stuff, and everybody knows you don't fancy it anymore."

Nitric acid off a duck's back. "Only," I observe, "Lofty's got a point. I could've ruined everything, blundering in not knowing it was a sleeper operation. If you want me to back off from the Third Horn, just say the word, and I'll go somewhere else."

He's got that harassed look I know so well. "What I want from you," he says, "is to carry on doing the job you were assigned to do and leave the long-term strategic planning to us. Just mind where you're putting your great big feet, that's all."

"Nothing would give me greater pleasure," I say gravely. "But it's no use saying don't go treading on the mines if I haven't got a map of the minefield."

I'm doing it on purpose, and both of us know it. I used to tease him back when he was just a snot-nosed junior executive officer and I was his superior, before I got all fragile and he was promoted into my warm, wet shoes. "Stay away from Brother Hildebrand, and you'll be just fine," he tells me. "There's sixteen other monks on his shift, go bother one of them. Talking of which," he adds, giving me what he fondly imagines is an intimidating stare, "what's all this about you handing out beatific visions like sweeties? You know perfectly well—"

I point out that I've already taken up far more of his valuable time than I could possibly deserve, and retire in good order, leaving him sullen and unhappy. Not, I hasten to add, intentionally. Just force of habit, I guess.

~

Something big involving a sleeper, an inside-man job. Ours, needless to say, is not to reason why, but inquiring minds want to know about things, and I have an inquiring mind. It's got me in trouble before now, and almost inevitably will again. Big deal.

That night, as I tickled the edges of one Brother Florian's consciousness with vague images of unimaginable transcendent wonder, I considered what I knew about various things: the political situation, the antecedents of Brother Hildebrand, the last recorded movements of various key players on both sides, one or two incidents from my own experience. I won't say a pattern started to emerge, but interesting shapes flickered in tantalizing fashion on the meniscus of the void, so much so that when I snapped out of it and looked round, I was alone in the chapel. There's always ten minutes or so between one shift clocking off and the next one filing in. It gives the vergers a chance to refill the lamps and do a spot of dusting.

It's just a job, that's all—a job for which we get no pay, no thanks, and a volcanic bollocking if things don't go exactly according to plan. We do it because that's who we are. You lot got free will; we were assigned our respective functions. We serve; therefore, we are. Furthermore (in theory, at least), every function in the divine service is of equal value, from archangels and cherubim down to night soil operatives and tempters. From each according to his ability, to each . . . Well, there is no *to*. We require nothing except work to do, which is provided for us, and we're supposed to be grateful.

Therefore, in the aftermath of the Unfortunate Event, there wasn't any punishment, as such. Perish the thought. Mercy and forgiveness are His middle names. What happened was that some of us who were doing jobs of equal value were reassigned to other jobs, also of equal value, jobs that the ones who chose the right side during the Event weren't awfully keen on doing, for some unfathomable reason. A minor adjustment in the great scheme of things, and the consensus of opinion is that we got off pretty lightly, all things considered.

True, no doubt. Even so.

Even before I was officially fragile, I relished (and

still do) the very occasional moment of quiet, stillness, and peace. Not something I tend to encounter in my everyday life. When I'm on the job—was on the job, pre-fragile—it's often quiet, sneaking around on tiptoe so as not to alert the householder to your presence, but the stillness tends to be the pre-storm variety, and you can forget all about peace. When you're deep inside the mind of the sort of people we generally get called on to inhabit—let's say I've been in some pretty grim places in my time, and nearly all of them have had bone walls. It's noisy in there, what with all the sobbing and the yelling and the horrible vivid memories played back at maximum volume, over and over again. One thing you can't do under such conditions is hear yourself think. The Third Horn chapel is, by comparison, an earthly paradise.

The leading feature of the chapel, according to all the books, is the Great Iconostasis. Forty feet high and twenty-three across, with a gold leaf background that turns into a sheet of flame when the late-afternoon sun streams in through the rose window at precisely the first verse of evensong, it depicts the Sorrow of the Mother, which has always struck me as odd and just a smidgen off-color, doctrinally speaking. Brother Eusebius explains it by saying that just as human mortals can't look directly at the sun without damaging their optic nerves, they can't directly address Him face-to-face and person-to-person without risking spiritual damage—

("It makes you go blind, in other words."

He grins at me. "Exactly.")

—so they seek the intercession of an intermediary, in accordance with the properly constituted chain of command: priest to guardian angel to archangel to principality to power to virtue to dominion to throne to cherub to seraph to Holy Mother and eventually to the big boss himself. It's all about proper channels, which proverbially run deep, and doing things the right way, so that everybody knows where they stand and the file copies end up in the right folders.

Color me unconvinced. I think it's something fundamental, part of your and our shared heritage. Throughout your history, and ours, we don't go to the king or the CEO or the governor of the province, because we're scum and we know it. No, instead we like to have a quiet word in the ear of someone who has the ear of the Big Man. As often as not, our hymn of supplication to the ear-haver has an instrumental accompaniment, the jingle of coins or the crackle of crisp notes, sweet music to charm the savage breast. It's the same rationale that worked so very well for Sighvat III. No point a creep like me asking for anything, but surely He'll listen to his own mother.

A creep like me. I slip unobtrusively into human form

(look closely, and you'll see a densely packed swarm of tiny flies; best not to look too closely) and kneel, telling myself it's okay, it's just a picture, a picture of someone who never actually existed, since He never had a mother. I should know, I was there a fraction of a second later, and besides, I'm not *praying,* perish the thought, just taking the weight off my feet. I'm not praying, because prayer is basically just asking for stuff, and I have no stuff to ask for. But it's nice, once in a while, to stop and have a breather and pretend, just for a fleeting fraction of a moment, that I'm not me.

A shadow falls between me and the shining gold vision. I look over my shoulder. Oh, for crying out loud.

He grins at me. "You're going to be in so much trouble," he says.

~

There's that moment in that play, when the hero comes upon the villain kneeling at an altar: "Now might I do it pat, now he is praying." Saloninus's hero is intriguing because he's indecisive. The caster of the shadow isn't like that at all. With him, to think is to act, only he very rarely thinks. He just does.

I can be quick when I need to be. I dissolve the borrowed molecules of my assumed human shape, scattering the swarm of flies like an explosion. Then I'm off, in every direction at once, like sound, but he's quicker. He grabs me. He's stronger than I am. He scoops me up in his hand and stuffs me into his ear.

~

We go way back, him and me, further back than I care to remember. This is the thing I said I'd rather not talk about, if you remember, but I'm going to anyway.

When I first met him—when I reminisce, unless I specify otherwise, *him* can only possibly refer to one individual for reasons you'll soon understand—I was only obeying orders. There's this child, says my district supervisor.

"Oh, come on," I say. "You know what they say about working with children and animals."

My supervisor doesn't like me much. "Tough," he says.

"Be a sport. Give it to someone else."

"Can't." He shakes his metaphorical head. "You were asked for specifically."

Wasn't expecting that. "You're kidding."

His edition of the big stone tablet has THOU SHALT NOT KID at number four. "Don't ask me why," he says. "I wouldn't choose you for anything if it were up to me, not if I wanted it done properly. But they specified you for this one, and that comes direct from upstairs."

Why am I not entirely overjoyed at this unexpected vote of confidence? "Fine," I say. "You'd better fill me in on the details."

Not the first time I'd possessed an unborn child; maybe that's why I got the job, because it's not the sort of assignment that comes up every day, and there are technical issues. A certain level of experience and expertise would, therefore, be useful. It's a long-term gig. If you go in that early, you can't come out again until the kid's at least five years old, not without killing it; besides, the whole point of going in before the subject's even been born is to create a really high-class munitions-grade sleeper, an ultimate inside man.

Ah well, not like I had anything better to do for the next twenty-thirty-forty years, and it was bound to be peaceful. No banging about, shouting, goading the subject into screaming fits, broken bones, acts of mayhem. Much more my sort of thing, because if you're designing and creating a long-term weapon, you want it to be well equipped, versatile, efficient, high performance; therefore, you want a cultured, educated mind in a strong, healthy body, with good social skills, an ear for music, a thorough basic grounding in the arts and sciences, theology and scripture and everything else a person might need in order to carry out an important mission, the particulars of which are to be announced later but which might involve *anything,* so best to be prepared. It was my duty, in other words, to turn the subject into as close as I could get to the perfect human; the Saloninan Übermensch; a compendium of all the qualities, skills, and virtues; the ideal weapon—

Great steaming heaps of ambiguity all over the place, of course, because the education and training he'd get from me would be practically identical to those lined up for the Saints. But that's the fundamental thing about tools and instruments, and weapons. They're neutral. A skilled craftsman makes them, then hands them over to the likes of you and me, who do things with them, nasty or nice, depending on which side we happen to be on. The nasty-nice dichotomy is, of course, a policy issue and way above my pay grade. I'm only obeying orders. Meanwhile, I get an opportunity to be a skilled craftsman, which is rather more my cup of metaphorical tea than what I'm usually called on to do, or lumbered with doing. As for this business of sides, the Divine Essence is best described as a perfect sphere, which is to say, a geometrical entity with no sides. Just various jobs that need doing, all of equal value.

So in I go, at the end of the tenth week, at which point brain activity has only just started; the roof's on and the paintwork is more or less touch-dry but in all other respects, vacant, to coin a phrase, possession. That's how it's supposed to be, at any rate, and medically and biologically, it's inconceivable that it should be anything else. I've done this sort of thing before. I know what to expect.

The prime directive of our order and Rule Number One: First, do no harm. If that sounds vaguely familiar to you, by the way, I'm not surprised. Your lot stole it from us, a long time ago. But we demons formulated our code of practice while the ancestors of your human doctors were still picking lice out of each other's fur.

First, do no harm: so I slide slowly and with infinite care through the upper layers of the unborn infant's mind, like a thoughtful husband easing into bed next to his sleeping wife. Doing no harm in this context means not letting the subject know he's being taken over. It's an incredibly traumatic thing for you people, to know you're being possessed. It's terrifying and you can't bear the intrusion—think what it's like when you've got a sharp bit of grit in your eye, and then consider how infinitely more sensitive your mind is, and how much more damage you can do by rubbing at it. But all your instincts scream at you to fight, and you're not to know that fighting us isn't actually possible. Really—don't try. The more you kick and thrash around, the more you bruise and break yourself, but you can't touch us, naturally. We aren't there, in your terms. We are spirit, essence, not of the body; not insubstantial, but composed of a kind of substance you could never even begin to understand. And if that sounds patronizing, you've missed the point. You really don't want to be in a position where you could begin to understand *us*.

The image I always use to describe that first stage is when a housewife pours a spoonful of rennet into a big, wide bowl of fresh milk. That's how I come to exist, in terms you might possibly be able to, no pun intended, get your head around. I *curdle* out of insubstantiality into substance. What I curdle, incidentally, is your brains, but the resultant mess isn't *me*. The knots and bogies of coagulated goop suddenly formed inside your head aren't me incarnate. They're still just proteins and fats and hemoglobin, the stuff you're made of. No, I'm the *process*, if that makes any sort of sense at all. When I go in, I catalyze, I set changes in motion. In Orthodox Trinitarian terms, there's now three of us in one: you, me, us. Or, to skip from one homely metaphor to another, your brain is an amorphous sludge of porridge and I'm the yeast. It's me that makes things interesting.

Gently does it. I drip through his consciousness slowly, like water through limestone, with a view to building stalactites in my own image, when I've got five minutes.

Then I see him. There absolutely shouldn't be any *him* yet for me to see. He sees me. Who are you, he asks, and what the hell do you think you're doing here?

It says in the code of conduct: Having effected a legitimate entry, an officer shall not desert his post unless relieved by a colleague, ordered to evacuate by a superior, or expelled by a duly authorized agent of the opposition. Desertion is a very serious matter, a court-martial offense, and if you're found guilty, the punishment is absolutely nothing at all, because what can they possibly do to someone like me? Break my sword and snip my buttons off? They already did that. Demote me and put me on light duties? Yes, please.

Accordingly, I back away toward the mouth of the eustachian tube, my preferred choice for a speedy getaway. He's quicker than me, and much stronger. He reaches out and grabs me. It's absolutely true that we can't be killed or even damaged, since we're immutable and not susceptible to any sort of change, while unending ages run. But we can feel pain. Boy, can we feel pain. He gets his fingers round my head, his thumbs in my ears, and squeezes. I feel pain. Lots of it.

When he's finished doing that, he lets go. "You're one of them," he says.

I stare at him. I'd assumed he was one of us. His appearance—but you can't judge by appearances, not when you're dealing with insubstantial beings. He sounds and acts like one of us. But apparently he isn't.

"Who are you?" I somehow manage to ask.

"Me? I live here."

Oh boy.

~

There's us, and there's them. You know by now who we are. They are our opponents: duly authorized officers of the Combined Service, whose job it is to expel us from the minds and bodies of human mortals, using words of command and the power vested in them, et cetera. Don't call them exorcists. They don't like it, and as a rule, they're not the sort of people you want to annoy.

In one sense, they're a parallel service to ours. In other respects, they couldn't be more different. For a start, they're all freelancers. Once they've qualified and got their tickets, they go out into the world and practice their vocation for money, usually a great deal of money. There aren't very many of them—it's not something you can simply decide to do, you have to be born to it, with the knack, a very rare gene, a mutation, not something that runs in families, like red hair—so demand for their services always outstrips supply, and the universal scientific principle of Survival of the Richest tends to direct their efforts toward possession victims in the higher income brackets. This is why, when you walk down the street, the crazy people you see frothing at the mouth and talking to people who aren't there tend to be thin and shabbily dressed.

I said just now that they're born with the knack. This

used to raise a whole symposium's worth of interesting questions: when does the knack actually kick in, and so forth. I can claim the honor of settling that issue once and for all. In some cases, particularly strong ones, it kicks in at some point before the end of the tenth week.

"You're one of them," he says.

He's knocked all my metaphorical teeth out. Since they're only metaphorical teeth, I can still manage to speak, just about. "How do you know that?"

He hits me. Then he jumps on my broken metaphorical ribs.

"How do you know," I wheeze—one of the broken metaphorical ribs has punctured my metaphorical lung, "about us?"

He shrugs. "Don't know," he says.

"Did someone tell you?"

"May have done." He stands on my metaphorical windpipe. "Why haven't you gone away?"

"You mean, why aren't I dead?"

"What's dead?"

Oh, for pity's sake. I tell him.

"Oh," he says.

"I'm not dead," I explain, "because we can't be killed. Just hurt a lot."

"You're bad."

"What harm did I ever do you?"

"You're bad. All of you are bad."

"If you say so. How do you know—?"

"Everybody knows that."

I nod—a neat trick with a metaphorical neck broken in two places. "Well," I say, "nice to have met you and sorry to have bothered you, and I think I'll go now." I start to drag myself to my shattered metaphorical feet.

He kicks me down again. "No, you don't," he says. "I haven't finished with you yet."

"Really?"

"You're bad. You're the *enemy*. Thou shalt not suffer a demon to live."

I close my metaphorical eyes, just for a moment. "First, I think you'll find that should be witches, not demons. Second, we can't die."

He glares at me distrustfully. "You say that," he says. "I don't believe you. You're bad. Bad people tell lies."

Now, about pain. For you lot, it's a useful and positive thing. It tells you when something's wrong with you. Admittedly, it's a bit naïve in believing that once you know about the problem, you can invariably put it right, so maybe as a system it could do with a little fine-tuning, and presumably they intend to do that in the Mark 2, which I gather is due for release anytime now, though for some reason my breath remains unheld. For us, it's a control mechanism. If you have on your books a large number of immortal, undamageable entities of dubious loyalty, you need some way of making them do as they're told, or at least that's the theory. They are, of course, missing the point completely. We aren't treacherous, and we never could be. We are His Divine Majesty's loyal opposition, and you can't get more loyal than that. Nevertheless, we come bundled with an array of very delicate, sensitive metaphorical nerve endings and a pain threshold so low it's practically underground. It means that the opposition, his lot, never have any trouble getting us to shift when they're serving notice to quit. Just the threat of what they're capable of making us feel is enough to get us out of there faster than an arrow from a bow—

"Please," I beg him, "stop doing that. It hurts."

"So what? You're bad. You're one of them."

"Yes, but I've surrendered. I give up. I'll go quietly."

I'm dangling by the metaphorical hair from his fist. "I don't care. I'm going to hurt you some more. Serves you right for being bad."

"Hurting people unnecessarily is bad," I point out. "Even if they're bad people. And if you do something bad, that makes you bad too."

"Unnessy—?"

"When you don't have to."

"I have to hurt bad people," he says. "It's my duty."

His spirit is ever so willing, but eventually his as-yet-unborn flesh grows weak. Worn out with honest toil, he stops for a nap. Very gently I prize apart his metaphorical fingers and extract myself from between them. Time to leave.

I'm halfway to the earhole when I stop and think about it. Remember what I told you about possessing an infant? Once you're in, you can't leave until they're at least five years old, not unless you want to kill them.

Do I want to kill the little horror? Need you ask?

But I can't. The prime directive of our order, Rule Number One: First, do no harm.

(Actually, there are two schools of thought about that. One scholarly faction disputes the reading, blaming textual corruption in the manuscript tradition. What it should say, according to them, is: *At* first, do no harm. Wait a bit, get yourself nicely settled in, and then roll up your sleeves and start laying about you with the poker. It's an entirely valid reading if you accept the textual emendation, and the philological evidence is ambiguous—a matter of personal choice, basically. Unfortunately, I made my choice a long time ago. I read *first*; no *at*.)

Yes, I urge myself, but just contemplate this monster and ask yourself: Will the world be a better place with him or without him? To which I give the only possible answer: Not my call to make. For all I know, the Plan has big things lined up for the little bastard to do. Nobody, especially a lowly field-grade officer like me, has the right to go fooling around with the weft of the great tapestry. Decision-making on that scale should be left to the proper authorities. They're on the fourth floor, incidentally, second level, the other side of the water cooler from the Department for the Regulation of the Fall of Sparrows: a dedicated, hardworking team who are passionate about what they do, and if you screw things up for them, they're on you like a ton of bricks. Besides, I tell myself, he's only a kid; he doesn't know any better. What he needs is someone to straighten him out, explain things, teach him the difference between right and wrong. There would be a certain irony if that person should turn out to be me, but no matter. Someone somewhere presumably knows what He's doing. Meanwhile, Rule Two: Thou shalt not second-guess the fourth floor.

~

"You're going to be in so much trouble," he says.

He'd taken the words right out of my mouth, except that at that moment, my metaphorical mouth was full of blood and loose metaphorical teeth, which I spat out onto the floor of his mind. Funny how the first thing he always does is smash my metaphorical teeth in. Force of habit, I suppose.

"Praying," he goes on, his voice giddy with delight. "That's blasphemy. You'll burn in hell for that."

"No, I won't," I say wearily. "And I wasn't praying. I was just admiring a work of art."

"On your knees."

"You get a better view of the brushwork that way."

"I saw your lips move."

"You did no such thing. They weren't lips, they were bluebottles. And I was not praying."

By now I should be able to anticipate his moves. Instead, I duck to the left and meet his metaphorical boot halfway. "You're the one who's in trouble," I pant.

"Really. How'd you make that out?"

"Unprovoked attack. Excessive force. I wasn't even inside anyone. You *abducted* me."

"You were engaged in extreme blasphemy. I exercised my discretion under section 6 and placed you in close confinement to avoid further desecration of a scheduled holy place." He stamps on my metaphorical ear. "Now I'm exercising my discretion under section 6a and pre-emptively preventing you from resisting arrest. Praying, for crying out loud. You should be ashamed of yourself."

"If I confess that I was praying, will you stop hurting me?"

"No."

"Fine. I wasn't praying."

Being inside his head again brings back memories, not particularly nice ones. I was in there for seventeen years. He was a late developer.

"Why are you doing this?" I ask after a longish spell of the same old same old.

"Because you're bad."

"Doing this isn't going to make me any better," I point out.

"You infested my body for *seventeen years!*" he yells at me. "From before I was *born.*"

"All of which time you spent beating me up."

"That doesn't make it any better."

Then something rather wonderful happens. At first I'm not entirely sure what is going on. I can feel the hand of constraint on me, but not his—gentler, but firm and insistent. He hasn't noticed, too busy stamping on my metaphorical fingers. Then we both hear it: a reedy, elderly voice reciting the approved formula for exorcism, only you mustn't call it that.

"I bid you depart," warbles the voice. "Leave this body and return to the foul place from whence you came. I command you, in the name of light, go back to the darkness—"

I'm out of there like a rat up a drain. He screams at me, grabs at my metaphorical feet, but the magic words are doing their job and doing it blissfully well. I catch a whiff of incense and burnt beeswax, which means I'm out, free and clear. As I uncurdle and gratefully dispel myself into the air, the last thing I see is Brother Eusebius's beautiful, kind face, smiling at me as though in benediction.

~

"It's all right," he says later. "I owed you one, after all."

I pass him the sesame-seed rolls. "You won't get in trouble, will you?"

"For casting out a devil from a poor, disturbed pilgrim? I very much doubt it. Last time I saw him, he was shouting something about lodging an official complaint, but I don't think anybody will take him seriously. We get a lot of unfortunate souls here who aren't quite right in the head."

"Thanks."

"You're welcome." He looks at me. "Why was he doing that?"

"Long story."

"I have plenty of time."

So I tell him the truth, but not the whole truth.

"Seventeen years," he says. "I can see his point."

I give him a dirty look. "*His* point."

"Oh yes." He nods. "I had you in my mind for a few seconds, and I was too busy looking at—well, what you showed me—to pay much attention to anything else. But—no offense—"

"None taken."

"It wasn't pleasant. Like an itch you can't reach, together with a sort of feeling, I can't really describe it...."

"Alien," I say.

He nods again. "The knowledge of something being dreadfully wrong. Like touching a slug or a dead body."

"You got off lightly," I tell him. "For most people, it's like being splashed with acid or mercury. And the brain is the most sensitive part of the body. More nerve endings there than anywhere else."

He tries very hard not to let the revulsion show. "I forgive you," he says.

"Thank you," I say gravely. "You're fighting a losing battle, but it's a sweet thought."

"So," he continues, "I can see that man's point. Having you inside his head for seventeen years—"

"Quite."

"Even though he was bashing the stuffing out of you most of the time, still, it can't have been pleasant for him. I can see where he might be resentful. It's the difference between victory and forgiveness. His entire childhood spent trying to scratch an unbearable itch." He gives me a thin smile. "It must be horrible for the itch, having fingernails dug into it, but it rarely gets much sympathy. You can understand why."

"Except from you."

"Ah. That's my job."

I stand up. The bell is ringing for compline. Duty calls. "Anyhow," I say, "thank you."

"As I said, I owed you one."

My turn to nod. "True," I admit. "But I did you a favor while trying to tempt you into sin. The fact you saw through me like a window is neither here nor there. You, on the other hand—"

"Quite." He gives me a gentle smile. "But you see, I'm so much better than you."

"There's that, of course," I say, and walk away.

~

I go through the motions, but it's hard to concentrate when you're looking over your metaphorical shoulder all the time. Knowing he was out there somewhere, after me, on my trail like a predator, makes disturbing the eternal rest of Sighvat III seem even more pointless than usual, and Brothers Fidelius, Benno, and Hamilcar have no trouble at all shrugging me off as they pursue their devotions. I'm not, in other words, doing my job to my usual exacting standards, and halfway through lauds, I get a snotty memo from Division telling me to pull my metaphorical finger out. Just what I need to cheer me up.

"Seems to me," says Division, scowling, "that you're probably more fragile than we realized. Maybe it's time to take you out of the field altogether. A short spell at HQ doing simple, undemanding admin—"

"I'm fine," I tell him, shuddering. "Really."

He looks at the report on his desk. "Says here you were caught praying," he says, "and then you had to be rescued by a monk. Hardly inspires confidence, does it?" He favors me with a ghastly smile. "No, if you ask me, what you need is a chance to get away from it all for a while, pull yourself together, doing nice, gentle, stress-free work of equal value where you can't balls anything up." His scowl darkens. "I'll be straight with you," he says. "We've cut you a fair bit of slack over the years, on account of, well, you know, but it can't go on forever. I've got the good name of the Division to think about, for one thing. Naturally, I have every sympathy for a brother officer damaged in the line of duty, but believe it or not, I've got other things to do besides explaining to Compliance why one of my people feels the need to seek the intercession of the Holy Mother. Report to the seventh floor oh-six-hundred tomorrow, they'll tell you what needs doing. And stay away from the Third Horn, understood?"

"Why?"

"Your sudden fatal attraction to masterpieces of devotional art," he says unpleasantly. "Clearly some of us need a little help with not being led into temptation."

~

There is, of course, no seventh floor. Instead, there's a variation on the theme of existence where a faint memory of what I used to be, more a caricature than anything else, drifts in and out of partial consciousness just long enough to compile duty rosters and docket monthly returns. It's all, they tell you, about efficiency. You don't actually need memories or a personality or an identity to do routine administrative chores; in fact, you're better off without them. No distractions. Just the job in hand, and the bare minimum of functionality necessary to get it done. You can see why we snigger behind our hands when we look at your paintings and frescoes of Hell. Is that how you perceive eternal damnation? Brimstone? You people simply don't have a clue.

~

Pull yourself together, he said. Oh boy.

The risk, when you're reduced to mere essential function for any length of time, is atrophy. If you don't use it, eventually you lose it. Actually, I can see why so many of my colleagues end up volunteering for clerical duties. The first things to go are memories, and I think I can safely say that all of us who backed the wrong side during the Unfortunate Event have things we'd like to forget: essentially, everything that ever happened between the first syllable of the Word and ... what's the date today? We'd prefer not to remember things after the Event, because they're all horrible, and things before the Event, because they remind—sorry, too weak a word—they rub our noses raw in what we've lost. Clerical work is as close as any of us can hope to get to death: oblivion, the untroubled dreamless sleep of the deskbound.

My problem is, I quite like being alive, in spite of everything. A wise man, probably Saloninus, once said that the beating of the heart, the action of the lungs, is a useful prevarication, keeping all options open. While there's life, at the very least there's being here, even if here is a shitheap. Not being here, even in a shitheap, is nothing at all.

On the other hand, as long as I was in this pitiful state, I was *safe*. He couldn't get at me, because there was nothing to get at, and he couldn't find me, because there was nothing to find. Even what he'd already done to me was neutralized, because I couldn't remember it. Am I pathetic? Well, yes. I offer no excuses. I was just glad to be out of harm's way for a while.

So there I am, collating figures from the monthly re-turns, when it's as though a door opens in a darkened room and light comes stabbing in. I feel like a lamp that's just been lit—suddenly full of life, but burning.

"Hello there," says Division, giving me that look of his. "Just thought I'd drop by, see how you're getting on. Feeling all right?"

"Not so bad," I mumble.

"Splendid. Not quite so fragile?"

"Me? Tough as old boots, you know that."

"Good, because I've got a job for you."

"Of equal value?"

"Very equal indeed."

It all comes flooding back—who I am, what I was, what I am now, the Unfortunate Event, *him,* every-thing—and I'm standing in a place I know well, though I haven't been there for ages.

"From here," says Division, taking in the panorama with a vague sweep of his arm, "they reckon you can see all the kingdoms of the earth. On a clear day," he says, frowning slightly. "That over there must be Perimadeia," he adds, pointing at Bos Sirene. "Of course, last time I was here, they really were all kingdoms. Now most of them are republics and military dictatorships."

I have this slight problem with heights, though for crying out loud don't tell anyone. "Breathtaking," I say.

"Can we go down now?"

"I brought you here," he continues, "because I think it's really important in our line of work to keep a sense of perspective. Don't you agree?"

"In a sense."

"Perspective." He fills his metaphorical lungs with clean, fresh air. "Up here, you can appreciate what really matters."

Yes, indeed: getting back to sea level as quickly as possible. "Absolutely," I say. "Look, was there something specific? Only I know how busy you are."

He turns on me. "You've been through a rough patch lately, we both know that. I've been asking myself, wouldn't it be better if you transferred to admin full-time? For the foreseeable future, at least."

Division exists outside sequential linear time, so for him, all the future is foreseeable. "It's a sweet thought," I say, "but on balance, I'd rather not." The word *balance* does unpleasant things to my metaphorical inner ear, and I wobble alarmingly. He grabs my virtual arm. "It's all right," he says, smiling pleasantly. "Even if you did topple and plunge headlong, flights of demons would rush up and break your fall. It's all part of the service."

"That's good to know," I say. "But I wouldn't want to be a nuisance to anyone."

He lets go of me and turns to admire the view. "Just

feel that breeze," he says. "I really like it here. Fancy a snack?"

"No, thank you."

"Just say the word."

"Not just now."

"Suit yourself." He picks up a stone, transforms it into a truffle, sniffs it, and puts it in his metaphorical pocket. "We need you to do a job for us."

"I think you mentioned it earlier."

"It's not—" He hesitates. "It's not a nice job."

"Somehow, I didn't think it would be."

"It's of equal value, goes without saying. But it's not going to be fun."

I sigh. "What have I got to do?"

"Which is why," he goes on, "I want to make it perfectly clear, you don't have to do it. If the idea doesn't appeal to you, just say the word and I'll rush through the paperwork and you can start a permanent admin assignment straightaway. We do care, you know."

Get thee behind me, Division, I say to myself. Actually, on second thoughts, no. Definitely not the sort of person you want behind you, particularly when you're on top of a mountain. "You know me," I say. "The original eager beaver. Just tell me what you want me to do."

"Good man." He beams at me. "Now then, this lunatic exorcist who keeps bothering you."

Far away in the distance, I can see the sun glinting on the gilded dome of the Third Horn. Right now, judging by the position of the sun, they'd be ringing the bell for nones. "What about him?"

He taps the side of his nose. "It's all a bit complicated, and there's some aspects I'd rather not tell you right at this moment, because then I'd have to kill you." He laughs. Official Divisional humor. "The point is, you and this character have what you might call a special relationship. Am I right?"

I draw in a deep breath. It's like trying to inhale cottage cheese. "You could say that."

"GenTacCom thinks that's something we can use to our advantage, in respect of certain operations. I won't bother you with the details, but it's an important and valuable part of the Plan. What we need," he goes on, gazing into the deep patch of low cloud currently obscuring our view of all the kingdoms of the earth, "is a great big gray area, if you follow me. A sort of moral no-man's-land."

"Always a useful thing to have by you," I say. "Sorry, I'm not really following any of this."

"We need to blur the boundaries a bit." He seems to be having a little trouble finding the right words. "You know, I think sometimes we see things a bit too cut-and-dried, in the profession. Us and them, you know, black and white—"

"Good and evil."

He scowls at me. "Yes, we're on opposite sides. But opposite sides working towards the same objective. It's like a pyramid."

"Is it?"

"Just like a pyramid," he says. "At the bottom of the pyramid, you've got two pairs of opposite sides facing each other, in a standoff, us against them. By the time you reach the top, there's no sides, just a point. That's how we see the Plan. And the two sets of opposing sides *support* the point, they're the solid base on which the point *depends*. Their mutual opposition makes possible the ultimate coming together in unity. Anyway, wasn't it Saloninus who said, 'That which is done out of love is beyond good and evil'?"

"He was a mortal," I point out. "And I've always thought it was one of those sayings that sound really good till you stop and try and figure out what it means."

He smiles bleakly at me. I am one of his people and the sheep of his pasture, but that doesn't mean I'm not getting on his nerves. "Sometimes," he says, "we have to look past our differences and see what we're really trying to achieve. And sometimes we can't achieve it unless we temporarily put those differences aside."

I gaze at him. "You mean collaborate."

"No, I don't mean collaborate," he snaps, and for a moment I can't help remembering how very far off the ground we are. "You're twisting my words, which really isn't helping." He stops, takes a deep breath, starts again. "Think about it calmly and logically. After all, what is conflict?"

"Excuse me?"

"Conflict," he repeats. "We all know it takes two to make a quarrel. Conflict is where two parties come together to sort out their differences through combat, with a view to reaching a definitive conclusion. It's a voluntary act of cooperation designed to achieve a positive outcome."

I think about *him*, twisting my metaphorical head through 180 degrees. He likes doing that, but so far, we don't seem to have come to any helpful conclusion as a result. "Where is all this leading?" I ask.

"I'm trying to explain, but you will keep interrupting. Your friend. The exorcist."

"Yes?"

"He needs a demon. One he can control." He looks at me. "That would be you."

"He *needs*—?"

Long sigh. "He has a job to do," he says. "He needs you to help him. So I'm temporarily assigning you to him. Sort of a medium-term secondment."

My metaphorical teeth are so tightly gritted I can barely speak. "Doing what?"

"He needs you to possess someone."

"What?"

"Oh, come on—you know what possessing someone means. There's a mortal human. You go in. You do your stuff. In this case, what he tells you to do."

You think you've heard it all. "*He* wants me to do this."

"Yes."

"That's crazy. His job is casting out demons. Casting them *in*—"

"Look." We've reached the end of his rope. "This has been authorized by Area and JoCenCom. You can do it, or you can look forward to eternity in admin. Your choice." Unpleasant grin. "Free will. It's entirely up to you. Only I need you to make up your mind *now*. Capisce?"

"Presumably he asked for me specifically."

"Oh yes. It's you or no deal. And it's important, to the Plan. It matters."

Wherein, I assume, lies the difference between it and me. The sheep of his pasture: his to shear, his to flay, his to roast on skewers. "Can we go down now?" I say.

~

The dog bites you, they say, because it likes you. I think he must like me, because the first thing he does is bite me.

With his actual metaphorical teeth—they meet in my

throat, he shakes me, then lets go. "You think you're so clever," he says.

"Do I?"

"Getting your monk friend to rescue you like that. So smart. You make me sick."

He smashes my metaphorical head against the wall of his skull, and for a moment it hurts so much I can't think. "Would it help if I say I'm sorry?"

"No, because you'd be lying. Why can't I ever *do* anything to you? I keep bashing away at you, and nothing *happens*." He twists my broken metaphorical arms behind my metaphorical back, and I scream. He clicks his tongue irritably. "Don't do that," he says.

"But it hurts."

"I don't believe you can feel pain. I think it's all just an act."

He's stronger than I am, in the same way that you're stronger than a newborn baby. He always has been. But sooner or later he tires himself out, and we have a brief respite. That's when my shattered bones knit, my dislocated joints realign, my ruptured organs mend, all ready for the next bout. "They told me you'd asked for me."

He nods, exhausted. He's slumped against the wall of his skull, pale and drawn with fatigue.

"Why me?"

"Because I know you. And you know what I'll do to

you if you try and piss me about."

"What do you want me to do?"

He gazes at me. I can feel him forcing himself to endure me without taking action. It's a real struggle for him. Think what it's like when you inadvertently touch a burning hot surface, the instant of yelping pain before you can get your hand away. Now imagine deliberately leaving your hand there. That's what it's like for him. I don't like him much either, but I never felt that intolerable, to-the-death, him-or-me loathing. I'd feel sorry for him, if it weren't against the rules.

"Have you ever," he asks, "been to Antecyra?"

~

The answer is, of course, yes. By an odd coincidence, it really is the last place He made—day six, when it was getting late and His mind was starting to drift toward other things, with consequences that will shortly become apparent.

Antecyra, as everyone knows, is the bleakest, hottest, most barren, least productive, most hostile, and most intensely desirable piece of real estate on earth. To the west, you have the Great Inner Sea, with the prosperous trading nations of the western islands a day's sail away across relatively peaceful water. To the north, you have the powerful but arriviste Robur, vulgar, violent men with more weapons than money. They came south from the distant steppes a few hundred years back, having been driven out of their ancestral grazing circuits by savages even more unspeakable than they are. There's an awful lot of them, and it's a stroke of luck for everyone else that He took the trouble to impede their southern border with a ridiculously tall mountain range, through which there are only two usable passes. To the south of Antecyra is the ancient, immeasurably strong, nearly brain-dead civilization of Blemmya, where they wrap embalmed cats in bandages and worship them as gods. Blemmyans aren't like normal people, and time passes very slowly there, but heaven help anyone who is perceived as threatening their mercantile or diplomatic interests. Finally, across the desert to the east, you have the Sashan, inventors of writing and agriculture and self-styled lords of creation. They build vast palaces in the middle of the sandstorm-scoured wilderness, decorated with colossal basalt friezes of war and lion-hunting. They believe that the world belongs to them, and all non-Sashan are trespassers.

Wedged in between these three nightmares, you have Antecyra. There's a ribbon of flat, fertile land beside the sea, and then the mountains rear up at you, and on the other side of the mountains, you have white, flat desert, in parts of which rain has never fallen. You can forget about sowing grain in Antecyra, apart from that narrow bit of seaside. The lower slopes of the mountains will just about grow vines and olives, and a few miraculously tough sheep wander about on the middle slopes; everything else is bare rock with a graceful, permanent garnish of snow. There are about seventy thousand Antecyrenes at any given time—nobody knows or cares precisely how many—and they make their living selling wine, olive oil, and wool to the Blemmyans, the Robur, the Sashan, and the Vesani, across the calm blue sea. It's not very good wine, oil, or wool, so they don't get paid very much for it. They have two mud-brick cities, Amphipolis in the north and the capital, Beal Regard, in the south, where the Duke lives.

Ekkehard VI of the House of Jaos is no better and no worse than his nineteen predecessors on the ducal throne. He's a man of limited intelligence and stunted imagination, a pragmatist, born and raised in the somewhat patched and faded purple. He knows that his tiny, piss-poor kingdom exists only because if one of his three appalling neighbors were to invade, the other two would immediately attack the invader, and there would ensue a war that would end only when the last man on earth killed the last-but-one and stuck his head up on a pike. He knows that every single thing he does is intensely scrutinized by three sets of spies, all frantically seeking to misinterpret his actions. He also knows that every last cupful of flour in Antecyra comes from abroad, so that if his merchants don't trade intensively with the people next door, all his subjects will starve to death within a year. The only remarkable thing about Ekkehard is that in order to get this particularly stressful and unrewarding job, he murdered four people, including two close relatives; since that's been standard operating procedure in the House of Jaos for centuries, nobody thinks anything of it, including him.

The trouble begins when a Vesani merchant, looking to get a few trachea in the nomisma off the tariff, gives Ekkehard a present. It's a book. It's a beautiful thing, written and illuminated on the finest cream-white vellum by the monks of the Golden Spire in far-off Perimadeia. The pages are framed with vine-and-acanthus borders on a background of gold leaf, and the pictures are little masterpieces—scenes of daily life, chivalrous warfare, courtly love, the Ascension—all the kind of thing they do so well at the Golden Spire. The cover is gorgeously embossed leather studded with small rubies and emeralds, the fleur-de-lis pattern tooling gilded in the incuse, and there's a silver-gilt clasp so beautiful it would break a heart of stone. Things like that, the abbot of the Golden Spire told the merchant, go down really well with primitives, whereupon the merchant ordered six and paid top dollar for them.

The merchant gives Ekkehard the book, and he's thrilled with it, though not quite thrilled enough to give the merchant his six trachea off; he says he'll have to think about it, which is no in dukespeak. No one's ever given him a book before. He takes it with him into his inner chamber and admires it, marveling at the vibrant colors, the exquisite grace of the shapes and patterns, the sensual textures against his fingertips, the rich smell of the leather, freshly rubbed with camellia oil from faraway Echmen. Then he does something that nobody, not even the deep thinkers on the fourth floor, could ever have expected him to do. He sits down and starts to read it.

Because Ekkehard can read, though not many people know this. It's his mother's fault. She realized that a lot of the papers shoved under her husband's nose for him to sign didn't actually say what the Grand Vizier said they said, and from time to time, bad things happened in consequence. So, without telling anyone, she hired a scribe to teach her son the dark art, impressing on both of them the necessity of keeping the secret strictly between themselves. Two decades later, when Ekkehard achieves the throne of his ancestors, he comes to appreciate the wisdom of his mother's decision, almost (but not quite) enough to make him wish he hadn't been compelled to put belladonna in her onion soup. When the Vizier brings him things to sign, he says, "Leave them there, I'll do it in a minute," and when nobody's looking, he reads them. No one suspects, and the aristocracy of Antecyra attribute his uncanny knack of sniffing out funny business to a pet demon, which he's reputed to keep in a jar by his bed.

It wouldn't have mattered if the book had been the usual sort of thing they churn out at the Golden Spire: missals; psalters; manuals of hours; nice, safe selections from the User's Guide that nobody bothers with very much, because they know the words by heart and have stopped thinking about them, the way a married man eventually stops listening to his wife. Ekkehard is a devout enough man after his own fashion. The harsh facts of his life mean he very much needs someone to pray to, and he's been told since childhood, this is what you do, and he's done it and he's still alive, so if it ain't broke, don't fix it. A pretty psalter would've been water off his spiritual back.

But this book isn't a psalter, or even a bestiary or *The Lives of the Saints*. It's Saloninus's *On the Genealogy of Morals,* which happens to be the favorite reading of a dissolute and rebellious monk at the Golden Spire. Called on to produce six luxury-grade illuminated codices at ridiculously short notice by the abbot, he grinds out five copies of Bononus's *City of God* and then falls into a sort of brown study. If he has to illuminate one more *City of God* or *Very Rich Hours* or anything like that, chances are he's going to lose all vestige of control and start stabbing people with his penknife. So instead, he retrieves his contraband one-volume edition of the *Genealogy* from under the loose floorboard in the scriptorium and sets about copying that instead. Inspired by the subject matter, he does a really bang-up job, finishing it off with sheets and sheets of gold leaf and extra sparklies on the cover. It doesn't matter, he tells himself. Nobody will ever know, because nobody ever actually reads these things.

So Ekkehard reads *On the Genealogy of Morals,* and strange things begin to happen to him—

~

(As it so happens, I met Saloninus once, not long after his death. Once he'd got his bearings and realized where he was and what had happened to him, and who I was, he gave me an enormous grin.

"You were wrong," I told him. "April fool."

He laughed. "Oh, that's all right," he said. "I was pretty sure I was wrong. Nice to have that confirmed, though."

I frowned. "You believed?"

"Unshakably," he said. "Ever since I was a kid."

"So why did you write—?"

"Money," said Saloninus. "I mean, nobody was going to pay to read about how He exists—there's a million books about that already. But a really convincing argument that He doesn't exist would be an instant bestseller. And it was. Flew off the shelves, scribes copying round the clock. Unfortunately, I was down on my luck when I was writing it, so I sold the rights to a man in Boc Bohec for twenty gulden. Pity about that."

I nodded. "A great pity," I said. "That book means there's a great many people round here who don't like you very much."

He looked horrified. "That's not fair," he said. "It's only a book."

"Quite," I said, lifting him up on the tines of my fork and pitching him into the everlasting bonfire.

Only a book. Me, I'd give anything to have written something like that, but that would be creation, which in my circles is a rigidly controlled monopoly. You may ask, incidentally, why the *Genealogy* is permitted to exist, since it's such a thorn in the Divine flesh. That would be missing the point. We aren't, after all, barbarians. We respect the mortal human urge to examine, analyze, and scrutinize the universe, and to express the findings. Contrary to what some ill-informed people would have you believe, we're passionately committed to freedom of speech. We don't burn books. Only the people who write them.)

~

Anyway, there's Ekkehard, closing the book, the tip of his forefinger sore from tracing so many lines of text. He feels rather like someone who's been reliably informed about a huge stash of treasure buried in a plague pit. On the one hand, he's seen the light. There are no gods, and religion is simply an artifact of human morality, which in turn is a blend of mental expediency and fashion, with about as much validity as a pewter nomisma. On the other hand, the only thing that unites his wretched people and gives them the strength to carry on living in their lethally marginal homeland surrounded by enemies is their faith. It doesn't occur to him to lie or dissemble. He knows his limitations: he's not a particularly good actor. He knows that if he tries to carry out his duties as chief priest and head of the church, it won't take people long to realize that he's just going through the motions, that he no longer believes. In that case, wouldn't it be better to tell everyone straight out? There is no God, we're on our own and always have been, and all temples and monasteries are closed with immediate effect and their substantial treasuries forfeit to the National Poor Relief Fund. . . .

Yes, he thinks, people would like that. The Antecyrenes believe, and their faith is the pillar that supports the roof of their world. But it hasn't escaped their notice that while they're struggling to survive in bad years, eating nettles and selling their firstborn children so they can afford to feed the younger ones and pay the temple tax, the priests swan about in purple vestments and eat three square, delicately seasoned meals a day. Make it all the priests' fault, and divert their enormous wealth (some of their enormous wealth; let's not get carried away) to feed the starving and the homeless, and we might just get away with it. The new message would be: we've survived against impossible odds, and all this time, when we thought it was because He was looking after us, we were looking after ourselves; therefore, we must be really special people, and even if there were any gods, which there aren't, we wouldn't need them. Hard to imagine anyone in Antecyra who wouldn't find that line of argument attractive.

He is, he realizes, trying to rationalize a choice he's already made, not for pragmatic reasons of statecraft but because he is who he is, he's seen what he's seen, and he can do no other. He cannot tell a lie—not one this big, anyway. Because the treasure's there, he has to dig it up, even if it means catching the plague—even if it means spreading it. Over the doorway of the throne room, his grandfather had an inscription carved in huge letters: ABOVE ALL, THE TRUTH. He's seen it at least once a day, every day of his life. Now, for the first time, he thinks he knows what it means.

He sends for the Grand Vizier. You're not going to like this, he says.

~

I stare at him. "This is terrible," I say.

"Who gives a shit what you think?" he replies, but doesn't hit me. He's preoccupied. If I didn't know him better, I'd say he's worried.

"This wasn't in the Plan, was it?"

"Shut your face."

"The Plan's all screwed up. This wasn't meant to happen."

"I told you to—"

"Oh, be quiet."

He doesn't hit me. I'd braced myself for the impact, which doesn't come, and I topple forward. He gives me a look that would've stripped rust off a shipwreck anchor, but no actual metaphorical fist in the face or boot to the kneecap. "I need to think," I say.

He doesn't reply. He's far away, trapped in the implications of the story he's just told.

"The hell with this," I say. "I need to talk to Divisional Command."

"You're seconded to me."

"I need to talk to Division."

He looks at me, bewildered. "There's no need to shout."

"Be right back," I say, and I'm out of there.

~

"All right, yes," Division concedes. Below us, all the kingdoms of the earth go about their dreary business. The pigs we've temporarily appropriated for our impromptu conference get on with the daily round of nosing up taproots. "There's been an aberration in the Grand Scheme."

"You mean it wasn't supposed to happen."

"No."

"But it did."

"Yes."

Getting a straight answer out of Division is a bit like mining lead. It's possible, but it's long, hard, noisy, dirty, dangerous, difficult work, and the result is generally poisonous and not worth having. "That's not possible," I say.

"True," he says with a sigh. "But it's a very old universe, and it's still got a very long way to go. And we run it, on

His behalf. And He's infallible, but we're—" He smiles weakly. "Not Him."

I close my eyes and count to five. "So how could this impossible thing happen?"

"Oh, easily enough." Now that the saber-tooth tiger is out of the bag, he's rather more relaxed than usual. "After all, we deal with mass effects, most of the time. We have to. We haven't got the staff for a truly tailored service."

I nod. My pig unearths a truffle and treads on it.

"Antecyra," he goes on, "was supposed to be inevitable. From the moment of Creation. By putting it there, He set in motion a sequence of events that could only have one possible outcome."

I can more or less see what he means. Antecyra, remember, was made on the sixth day. He'd already made the vast, alluvium-rich river that would ensure Blemmya would always be a superpower; the northern steppes, where the conditions of life must someday breed a nation like the Robur; the mighty twin rivers that ensured that Sashan would inevitably be the cradle of civilization. And then he plonked Antecyra down at the place where the three soon-to-be crucial nations must eventually collide and, for good measure, he made it very horrible to live in. Then all He had to do was step back and let human nature take its course.

"Antecyra is the whole point of the exercise," Division

goes on. "The Antecyrenes are His chosen people, though perhaps 'picked-on people' might be more appropriate. Anyway, they're what you might call the anvil of the Plan, on which He will forge the elements of the True Way."

Made sense. The anvil of his Plan—and what happens to anvils? They get bashed on. Getting bashed on is what they're for.

"And the same goes," he says, "for Antecyra. Think about it. What's the common experience of ninety-nine percent of human mortals throughout the full extent of sequential linear time? Answer: doing the best they can to survive in a hostile, unforgiving world; continually threatened and brutalized by forces they can neither control nor resist; born to trouble as the sparks fly upwards; inured to defeat, loss, and humiliation; dragging through their nasty, short, brutish lives with KICK ME painted indelibly on their backs. I mean, what would be the point of choosing the Robur or the Sashan? They're natural winners, they'd have entirely the wrong expectations, they'd be bitterly disappointed, and Faith would go down the toilet. And if you gave ten commandments to the Blemmyans, they'd obey them to the letter at all times without question, which would prove nothing. So, when drawing up the Plan, He organizes everything so as to lead to the Antecyrenes' existence, because they're serial victims and perpetual losers, the epitome, the archetype of human life on earth. Accordingly, to them He will in due course reveal the Way, and they of all people will understand."

I nod again. "Good plan."

"Yes, it is. It's just a pity it should all go tits up on my watch."

We sit in silence for a moment, contemplating the enormity of it all. "You're going to be in so much trouble," I point out.

"Yes."

"I don't suppose there's any way you can misrepresent the facts so as to make it look like it's somebody else's fault?"

"I thought about that," he replies, "but sadly, no."

"Have you considered going to your superior officer, telling him everything, and trying to find a constructive way forward?"

"Are you out of your tiny mind? Of course not. We've got to fix this ourselves, it's the only way. Otherwise, it's just going to get worse and worse, until when eventually it hits the fan, we're all going to wish we'd never been created. You included."

"Me? What did I do?"

"Having nothing to do with it is no excuse, you know that. Anyway, now you know, and I'll be very much obliged if you'll keep all of this strictly to yourself."

"Of course."

"Thank you."

I hesitate, then ask: "Where does *he* come in?"

"Ah. That's the supreme buggerment. Your pal was the one who spotted the problem first and reported it to Regional. Regional told me, and here we all are. He's involved, unfortunately, and if we want to keep his mouth shut, he's got to be involved. Or should I say implicated? And if he's involved, then so are you. Sorry about that," he adds.

I take a deep breath. "I understand," I say.

~

I pause on the threshold of his ear, amazed that he isn't aware of me. I clear my throat. "Honey, I'm home," I say.

Nothing. So in I go.

I find him slumped against his skull wall, metaphorical elbows on metaphorical knees, metaphorical head in metaphorical hands. I've never known him like this.

"I'm back," I say.

He looks up at me. The loathing is still there, but the look is different. I'm no longer the worst thing in the world. Something even ghastlier has supervened.

Outside, a ship is cutting the still blue water of Beloisa Bay. We're on it, en route from Beloisa to the ancient, fabulously wealthy merchant island of Scona, for two thousand years the commercial bridge between East and

West. Our cargo is ivory, apes, peacocks, sandalwood, cedarwood, sweet white wine, and all that kind of stuff. From Scona, at this time of year, it's just over a day's sail to Amphipolis on the Anticyrene coast. There, the ship will off-load its ballast, seventy tons of last year's barley, turfed out to make way for the new harvest but a valuable commodity in Antecyra, and take on two hundred jars of sub-prime olive oil and forty bales of coarse wool, before continuing on its stately coast-hugging way to its real destination, the Blemmyan port of Naucratis.

"Oh," he says. "It's you."

"I had a useful talk with my people at Divisional HQ," I tell him, "and you'll be pleased to know that they're right behind your proposed course of action a hundred and ten percent, and we're all officially working together for the duration of the emergency and singing," I can't resist adding, "from the same hymn sheet. Division recognizes," I add, as he stirs ominously, "that this is an unprecedented development for both of us, and you must be feeling apprehensive about it, to say the least, just like we are. However, they wanted me to highlight the uniqueness of the circumstances and the importance to both of us of getting this thing sorted out, and to thank you once again for your willingness to put your personal feelings on hold for the good of the mission."

He springs to his metaphorical feet, smashes me to

the ground, and grinds his metaphorical heel in my metaphorical ear until something breaks. So that's all right. He's feeling better now.

~

In theory, it's very difficult to get an audience with the Duke of Antecyra. You have to apply to the Lord Chamberlain, and you can't just walk up to him in the street and say, *How about it?* In order to get an audience with the Lord Chamberlain, you need to apply to the Deputy Equerry, whose diary is managed by the Lesser Comptroller of the Bedchamber, who can be contacted through the Office of the Count of the Stables, who employs seven clerks, each of whom has to be approached in turn. In practice, there's a handy one-bribe-pays-all fast-track system, essential in a mercantile nation where overseas bribes are a major source of desperately needed hard currency.

As we pass through the streets of Beal Regard, I can't help noticing a change since the last time I was there. The bazaars are still uncomfortably crowded, the pavements still too narrow, the buildings too tall and badly in need of repair and maintenance, and the smell is as bad as ever, but the people have changed. They're quieter. They don't shout. They mutter. I get the impression of thirty thousand people cooped up in a confined space, waiting for something to happen—bad or good, they don't know, but they're realists with functional memories.

A poor mad beggar lurches in front of us, takes one look at my pal, and scuttles away up an alley. In that one look, whom do I see but my old comrade in arms, Lofty, last seen possessing the outskirts of the mind of Brother Hildebrand, back in the Third Horn monastery. I can't do more than wave and mouth *Hello, Lofty, what are you doing here?* for fear that *he* might notice, see Lofty inside the beggar and waste valuable time and energy tearing my esteemed colleague limb from metaphorical limb; for his part, Lofty gives me a ferocious scowl, signifying *You don't know me, you didn't see me, I'm not here.* Interesting. Has Lofty been assigned to be—Saints and ministers of grace defend us—my backup? Desperate times indeed.

The palace gate is at the end of a street indistinguishable from any of the other streets in Beal Regard: too narrow, the buildings too tall, the pavements lined with too many ramshackle stalls selling underdeveloped vegetables and assorted stolen goods. It suddenly looms up at you, like it's going to hit you. It's about a thousand years older than the street below it, and a thousand years ago, the Dukes of Antecyra either had a bit more spending money or were less conscientious about paying stonemasons, because the gate is flanked by two colossal figures: bodies of lions; legs of eagles; heads of crowned, bearded humans. The paint has all flaked off and they're a bit the worse for wear these days, and they were never exactly wonderful, being one-third-scale knockoffs of the appallingly vast Gates of Acbadan in the Sashan Highlands. In context, however, they're quite effective. Someone important lives here, they intend to convey, and they do it pretty well. They're defended against all comers by two soldiers, recently up from the country. They glare at us.

"I'm expected," my pal says.

They give him a suspicious look. One of them opens a sally port in the main gate, nips through, comes back a few moments later with a fat man in a grubby quilted vest covered in rust stains; he's the officer of the day, and can read. "Documents," he says.

My pal shows him a bit of broken pot—paper is expensive in Antecyra—on which the Deputy Equerry has written our safe conduct. He scowls at it and tells the soldiers to let us through. The easy part.

The Lord Chamberlain looks at us. "Don't I know you?" he says.

My pal shakes his head and says, "I don't think so," but he's lying. There's a memory—third shelf up, seventh ledger from the right—of something inside the Lord Chamberlain's head that shouldn't be there, and for the first time I see one of us the way my pal sees us. It's horrible. It's a sort of monstrous crustacean, with scales and claws, round black eyes, a perfect circle for a mouth, two concentric irises of razor-sharp chitin for teeth. Is that how he sees me? It makes my flesh creep.

~

(It's a brief memory. The Lord Chamberlain is about seventeen, and he's vaguely aware that he's been acting funny lately. He's had fits in the street, he shouts a lot, in a language he doesn't understand. There's something lodged in his mind, like a stray fiber of bacon wedged between your teeth, and it shouldn't be there; most of the time it just itches unbearably, but sometimes it stings and sometimes it burns, and when he's doing the weird shouting, there's a pain like someone standing on your broken arm—I sympathize—and the only way to make the pain stop is to shout louder, except that it doesn't, it makes it worse. My pal scoops all of this out of his mind like a dredger as he confronts the intruder, a very junior officer I haven't seen in ages.

"Get out," my pal says.

"Just going," replies the junior officer. He gets up to leave.

"One moment." My pal bars his way. Here we go, I say to myself. "That crazy lingo you had him spouting."

"Ancient Luvian," says the junior officer.

"It's a real language?"

"Oh yes. Extinct now, of course. I made him recite the Benediction backwards in it."

"Why?"

The junior officer shrugs. "Orders," he says. "I just do as I'm told. Can I go now?"

My pal draws aside the hem of his metaphorical garment to let him pass. He doesn't even rabbit-punch him on the way out. Very efficient, very civilized. Just another day at the office.)

~

"I'm sure we've met before," the Lord Chamberlain says.

"Anything's possible," my pal replies. "But if it were anything important, I'd remember."

And so into the presence. I didn't exactly get my hopes up, which is just as well. The throne room, absolute pinnacle of magnificence in Antecyra, is about two-thirds of the size of the small cloister at the Third Horn, with plain brown and white tiles on the floor, two rows of six skinny columns holding up the featureless ceiling, plain whitewashed walls, and, at the far end, a throne; that is to say, a fancy-looking armchair in a sort of dark wood, decorated with crudely carved panels that were probably sold to the King's grandfather as ivory but which are in fact walrus tusk.

On either side of the throne stand soldiers with spears and shields but no helmets or breastplates, which cost money; behind it and to the left, an elderly man in a plain white gown, presumably the Grand Vizier. On the throne is Ekkehard VI, the man who's derailed the sublime Plan and made all this trouble and extra work for the hosts of heaven and the Princes of Darkness. He looks like a tradesman; if asked, I'd have said a carter, possibly a night soil collector, definitely someone who works with horses. His hair is combed over a bald patch, and he has a front tooth missing—top row, middle.

He looks at my pal and sees the merchant's red silk gown with the fur tippet, the poulaine-toe shoes, the broad-brimmed beaver hat. He could never afford to dress like that himself. "What do you want?" he says.

My pal digs me in the metaphorical ribs. "I'm going, I'm going," I say.

—And a fraction of a second later, I'm there when Ekkehard loses that tooth. It's in a friendly scrap with the stable boy, who's bigger and stronger and much faster, but who tries to pull his punches because his opponent is the Duke's son. He does his best, but young Ekkehard has never got the point about keeping your guard up; the stable boy throws a fairly anemic left hook, designed to miss, and the future father of his country walks straight into it. Down he goes, and he contrives to land just so on the cobbled yard, and he picks something up, and it's one of his own teeth.

I put the memory back where I got it from and look around. Don't tell anyone, for crying out loud, but I have a problem with confined spaces, which is why Ekkehard's mind gives me the shivers. It's very confined in here: narrow, cramped, no room to breathe. Easy, tiger, I whisper to myself. If I start panicking, he'll notice, and all hell will break loose.

Ekkehard is talking to my pal about something. I'm not really listening, but I catch the odd phrase about excise duty and premium-grade pickled herring FOB Scona and there not being much call back home for that sort of thing. I never knew my pal could act. He's doing a very creditable impersonation of a Boc Bohec merchant, probably based on someone whose head he's been inside at some point. The Duke is paying attention, fondly believing that there could be money in this somewhere. I leave them to it.

~

I distinctly remember telling them all, back in the day. It'll all end in tears, I told them.

But they wouldn't listen, and they went ahead, and the rest is theology. The memories are sharp as razors in my mind: razors that I carelessly leave lying about and cut my-self on, fumbling in the dark cupboards of my memory for some recollection temporarily mislaid. I remember our ridiculously complicated attempts at security—how do you conspire against the Omniscient?—passwords and coded messages and passing secret information in plain sight. We were clowns. We deserved to lose.

What never occurred to us, the Firstborn of Light and Sons of the Morning, was that we were *supposed* to rebel, right from the Word go; it was part and parcel of the Plan, right from day one. We only figured it out later, after we'd been lined up in the exercise yard with our hands tied be-hind our backs and numbers hung round our necks, be-ing counted by the camp commandant.

Even you mortal humans can grasp the simple truth that went over our heads like a flock of migrating geese. What was the first thing He did? Let there be light. And as soon as you have light, you have its inevitable oppo-site: the absence of light, the places where the sun don't shine. Not being stupid, He knew precisely what the con-sequence would be, but He went ahead and did it any-way. He didn't actually say, Let there be darkness, but it was very strongly implied, you bet.

Hence the need for what I think I've already described as His loyal opposition—us. He faced a quandary, the first of so many rocks He's made that are so heavy He can't lift them—not without a lever, or cheating. He couldn't turn to a contingent of the heavenly host and say to them, Go away and be evil. But the job had to be done, and someone had to do it.

There was always an undercurrent of dissent, of course, right from the beginning. Never, it goes without saying, *Should we be doing this?* Unthinkable. But *Should we be doing it this way?* Rather more thinkable, and some of us began to think it. Again, not *Should He be doing it this way?* Perish the thought. Pronouns matter. No, it was in the delegated tasks, the actions performed through the agency of deputies and ministers—a billion percent loyal to Him personally, you understand, but with certain reservations about whether what some of His agents were doing truly represented His will.

I well remember the first time one of us (no names, no pack drill; up till that point, he'd been a respected and trusted member of the upper echelon) stood up in the middle of a team meeting and started to criticize the actions of a fellow officer. He'd barely started his remarks when he glanced up and saw the look on His face, whereupon he got a fit of the stammers, turned a funny color, and sat down again.

Nothing was said, of course, but shortly afterwards, he was reassigned to work of equal value, and a sort of chill went through the rest of us. Could've been me, we said to ourselves; I've often thought the same thing, exactly what he was trying to say, and look what happened to him. This isn't—

We searched for a word to define what this wasn't, and very reluctantly were forced to the conclusion that only one word would cut it. This isn't right, we said to ourselves.

Is it cheating to use a lever to lift a rock? I guess it depends on the circumstances.

~

I've been inside a lot of heads, of all descriptions and classes of people, but kings don't come my way every day of the week. There are, let's say, points of interest. There are similarities, which are interesting, and differences, also interesting. Uneasy, according to Saloninus, lies the head that wears a crown, and it's not hard to see why. For a start, it's crammed to bursting.

For one thing, there's generally a whole lot of education. His Royal Majesty's royal father, who started out as a goatherd in the Telmessus before joining the army, working his way through the ranks and leading a military coup, wants his son to have all the advantages he never had. Or, if His Majesty was born in the purple, no sooner is the screaming newborn out in the fresh air than they're on him like vultures—tutors in language and literature, history, geography and philosophy, the arts of war and the arts of peace—because that's the way it has to be and that's the way it's always been done. Normal kids don't get stuffed with all that junk.

Then there's a vast assemblage of other people's problems. It's a universal human belief (which our lot on both sides of the fence have probably not done enough to counteract, if truth be known) that everything that happens must be somebody's fault. In a monarchy, ultimately that somebody is the King. It's his fault because he did it; or he ordered it to be done; or he allowed it to be done; or he neglected to forbid it to be done; or he failed to envisage that it might be done; or he didn't do it, order it done, or allow it to be done; or forbade that it should be done; or never knew about it in the first place.

Nine times out of ten, of course, it really is his fault, but one time in ten is still a lot of times, when you add them up over the years. And sooner or later, every problem there is, whether domestic or foreign, ends up with the King. He may not give a damn. He may tell his ministers to clear all those people out from outside his door and get all that stupid paperwork off his desk, because it's a sunny day and he's going fishing. It's still all there, on the edges of his vision, in the back of his mind, like mosquitoes or toothache or one of us.

Then there's his own problems, many of which are just

like yours and mine—will it ever stop raining, am I starting to go thin on top, is my wife having an affair, where did I go wrong bringing up my children, is that recurring pain just heartburn or am I going to die?—and others of which are job-specific and go with the territory: Is X plotting against me? Will Y invade? How the hell are we going to make people believe we can fix the balance of payments deficit? Above all, how do I know if what I'm planning to do is sensible or incredibly stupid when nobody I ask dares give me a straight answer?

A mind like that is too busy to notice something like me. It recognizes that something's very wrong, but so what, something's always very wrong around here. Having a mind like that would be like walking through a snake pit barefoot and blindfold—there's nowhere safe to put your feet. Too many things you might bump into: the realization that one day, inevitably, it'll all go to hell and the enemy will invade or the people will rebel, and when it happens, there'll be nothing you can do; the look in your mother's eyes as she puts down her spoon and stares at you, having detected the unfamiliar taste in her soup; sealing the docket for the execution of your most trusted friend, who was prepared to murder you for not all that much money. Inside a head like that, everything hurts, so what's one more little thing, like me? I could live somewhere like that indefinitely; I could live, so to speak, like a king. The danger would be that I'd grow so fat I'd get stuck on my way out, like the bear in the children's story.

But I'm here with a job to do, and we're on a schedule. I'm here to gnaw my way into the brain stem and send this poor fool writhing and frothing at the mouth, preferably at the most solemn moment in an important public occasion, an all-too-visible demonstration of what happens to you if you apostasize and say nasty things about the one true faith. For obvious reasons connected with free will, the good guys can't do this. It would be the ultimate betrayal of the bargain sealed with an apple pip, back when the world was young. But if a demon happens, in the ordinary course of business, to possess a man who happens to be an apostate duke (now, there's a coincidence), and a holy man happens to be passing and simply does his job, with the unintended consequence that the apostate forsakes his foolish ways and returns to the faith—then good work all round, no rules broken or even visibly creased, everyone's a winner. Furthermore, no risk whatsoever of anything going wrong, because the demon in question is so demoralized and terrified of the holy man that he wouldn't dare pull any funny business, even if he was minded to, for fear of what would happen to him once he came out again. That, I think, was what sold the idea to their equivalent of Division. This guy, the pitch ran, is completely tame. Practically a pet.

Definitely a snake pit, and such big, plump, jittery snakes. When the time comes—I'm thinking the moment in the Ceremony of Keys where the Duke is surrounded by all the nobility of the kingdom, kneeling to do obeisance—I'll be able to whip up a real tornado in here, with all this stuff. I can't say I enjoy my work as a rule, but even a reluctant craftsman is hard put to it not to feel a certain satisfaction when he does his job really well, judged by the most exacting criteria of his peers. Should I make him break his own bones, or pluck out one of his own eyes? The latter would be symbolically resonant—his eye offended him, so he plucked it out—but I think my pal might be upset if I damaged the hardware significantly. It would reflect badly on him, he would be inclined to think, so I'd catch it from him later. So, froth, scream, writhe, speak in tongues, maybe assault a few of the landed gentry, and then on my way rejoicing, back (with any luck) to the Third Horn for some more cozy chats with Brother Eusebius. All stuff I can do standing on my metaphorical head.

I pause. Something's wrong.

Surely not. But, as Saloninus says, once you've eliminated the impossible, what remains, however improbable, must be the truth. I freeze and listen. Absolute silence.

You can hide and hold your breath, but you can't ever do anything about the smell. The stink, or odor or fragrance, is always a dead giveaway: sulfur and brimstone and all things nice, it's how you people know we're there, or so I'm told. Naturally, my metaphorical nose has long since tuned out my own smell, so the faint perfume of rotten eggs in vinegar isn't me. I analyze it further.

"Lofty?" I say.

"Keep your voice down, for crying out loud," Lofty hisses, loud enough to wake the dead.

"*Lofty?*"

A metaphorical hand shoots out from the shadows, grabs me, and pulls me into a dark corner, a crevice formed by the junction of the frontal, temporal, and parietal lobes. It holds me in a grip of iron. "Go *away*."

"I can't, you're holding on to me."

The grip relaxes, but I stay where I am. "You shouldn't be here," I say.

"*You* shouldn't be here."

One thing's for sure. If we both stay there hissing at each other, it won't be long before the host becomes aware of us, and a moment or so later, he'll be bringing the roof down. If that happens, too early and fatally disrupting the schedule, my pal out there will flay me alive and Division will be seriously annoyed. If, on the other hand, I abandon my post and leave, my pal out there will flay me alive and Division will be seriously annoyed. Unless, of course, I break the habits of an everlasting lifetime and do something intelligent.

"Fuck you, Lofty," I whisper, and leave.

~

Oh, the Plan. Always the Plan. Ask any of us what we truly believe in; the Plan, we say. Of course there's a plan, whole and indivisible, immortal, eternal, infinitely complex and wise. Only, I have my doubts.

I first wondered about the Plan way back when, in the old days, before you-know-what. At the time, I'm on special duty, seconded to the Tempter's office. Nice work if you can get it for someone of my temperament—it's out of the office, and it allows a certain degree of unsupervised action, a chance to use a little initiative.

So there I am, walking to and fro in the earth, and I get wind of a certain mortal human, a true believer. Everything this character does is right and in accordance with the Law, in spite of or because of which, he's rich, healthy, happy, and content. His charity knows no bounds, and everyone who comes into contact with him benefits as a result, but this doesn't in any way decrease our friend's bankroll; in fact, it increases it, because he's such a wonderful guy to do business with. This is the sort of man priests point to and say: *Told you so, it really works.*

So I go back upstairs, and it's time for the weekly staff

meeting, during the course of which He happens to mention His servant whatsisname, the happy rich guy, the poster boy. My most faithful servant, He says, casting a sideways glance at certain members of the heavenly host who may not have been pulling their weight lately.

"Of course he is," I pipe up. "Why wouldn't he be? You've given him everything he could possibly want."

He frowns. "Why shouldn't I?"

"Absolutely," I agree. "All I'm saying is, take away the goodies, and see how faithful this clown is then."

You could hear a pin drop. The divine countenance darkens. "You think so."

"Human nature," I say.

"Fine," he snaps. "Let's try it and find out."

I won't bore you with the whole story, which is long and discreditable to all concerned (except for me, as I'm only doing my job). It ends with the poor believer confronting Him and asking: *Why?* To which He can find no better answer than, Where were you when I laid the foundations of the earth? Which is no better than a parent saying to a kid, Because I say so. It's a mess. He tells the agonized, boil-covered human that all his suffering is because of the Plan. Of course, *there is no plan.* Instead there's me, doing my day's work in the Tempter's office and doing it exceptionally well—so well that I tempted Him and won.

Which is why, when my idiot colleagues start whispering in corners and saying, *This isn't right,* I can't find it in my conscience to refuse to join them, let alone turn them in to the authorities, even though I know perfectly well that their enterprise is doomed to failure and it'll all end in tears, especially mine. I can't bring myself to believe in the Plan anymore, because I happen to know, for a fact: there is no plan. Why there isn't one, I don't presume to know, and no doubt He has his reasons for not having one. But there is no plan. Here I stand, therefore. I can do no other, God help me.

~

There's never a pig around when you need one, so I slide in through the ear of the nearest camel and wait for him. I don't have to wait long.

"Listen," I say. He freezes, fist drawn back. "What?" he says.

I tell him. He stares at me. "That's impossible."

"Go and take a look for yourself," I tell him. "And while you're at it, get him out of there, if you can possibly do it quietly. And then perhaps you'd come back and tell me what's going on, because I haven't got a clue."

He's longing to hit me on general principles, but he somehow manages not to. "I don't trust you," he growls. "What're you playing at?"

"Oh, for pity's sake."

"All right, I'm going."

He stumps off. I amuse myself for about ten minutes, filling the camel's minuscule brain with music—Procopius's Ninth Symphony, for what it's worth—and am only mildly disappointed when the stupid creature goes straight to sleep. I look about me. Material culture changes slowly in very hot countries, I've noticed; you stick with what works, or you fry. All around me, His chosen people are buying and selling, mostly getting the rough end of the deal. Labor-intensive bulk commodities, which foreign traders can generally get cheaper somewhere else. I wouldn't want to live here even if you paid me.

He comes out of the palace. He's acquired, I notice, a black eye. "They won't let me see him."

Behold a man talking to a camel. Fortunately, not an uncommon sight in Beal Regard. "They want another bribe."

"Yeah. Bastards."

"Have you got any money left?"

"No."

I turn a handful of gravel into gold. It's an easy trick to do. He scowls at it, full of disapproval. "That's black magic," he says.

"An abomination," I agree. "Men have sold their souls for less. Considerably less, when I'm doing the negotiating." Stupid thing to say, and he exercises considerable restraint in not hitting me. "Should be enough for your pal the Vizier, though. If not, there's plenty more where that came from."

He takes a scrap of cloth from his sleeve, wraps it round his hand, stoops, and picks up the gold. "I'm only touching this stuff under protest."

"Noted."

All this time, it occurs to me, Lofty's in possession, doing whatever it is he thinks he's doing. "I'll need to take this to a goldsmith," he growls. "Stay there. Don't go wandering off, or I'll do you."

~

Which leaves me just enough time for a quick conference with Division. Would that count as wandering off? I ask myself. No, because I know exactly where I'm going, which is hardly wandering.

"You shouldn't be here," he says, peering at me over the rims of his metaphorical spectacles. They're a complete affectation, of course, since he sees with the inner eye. But he's handed me the perfect feed line, so I forgive him. To forgive is divine, but nobody's looking.

"I'm not the only one who's where he shouldn't be," I tell him, and make my report. His metaphorical jaw drops. "Oh nuts," he says.

"I take it you don't know about this."

He gives me a foul look, presumably because I'm there. "No, I do not," he snaps. "Well, all right, then. There's an accredited exorcist on-site. Get the little bastard out of there, pronto."

I pause before answering, to give him time to reflect. "Something tells me," I say slowly, "that Lofty being in there isn't just a coincidence."

"Don't be stupid. Of course it is." He's unconvinced. Worried. "It's just some idiotic seventh-floor cock-up, the left hand not knowing what the right hand's doing. Accordingly, the left hand had better pull its finger out, before everything goes to GHQ in a handcart." He scowls at me. "Make it so," he says, doing his best to sound like a senior officer.

"I don't think so."

"You don't think so, I see." He takes off the metaphorical glasses, folds the arms carefully, and puts them on his desk. "Any particular reason?"

"I know Lofty."

"So do I. Known him for absolutely ever. He was the seraph i/c beatific visions when I was first promoted to field duty, before the—"

"Yes," I say. "And Lofty's a good officer. Better," I acknowledge, though it burns me to do so, "than me, when it comes to getting the job done quickly and efficiently.

He doesn't make mistakes."

Division grins. "What, never?"

"Well, hardly ever. Not *big* mistakes, anyhow. If he's going to possess somebody, first he goes to Area and checks that it's all okay, particularly for someone high-profile, like a king or a duke. And surely something like this would've been flagged up at Area."

He looks thoughtful. "You'd have thought so," he concedes, "though I don't know. They're the biggest bunch of deadheads unhung, a lot of the time. But, no, you're right, it'd have rung alarm bells."

"Also," I go on, "Lofty isn't blessed with an infinity of initiative. Or, come to that, imagination. If he simply needed to clock up some possession time to make his quota, he wouldn't choose a *king*. Definitely," I add, "not the Duke of Antecyra."

"No, I suppose not. So, what are you suggesting? He's part of the Plan?"

"He's part of *a* plan. Not necessarily the one we're part of."

Division groans. "Oh, come on," he says. "That's going too far. This is all second-archer-on-the-grassy-knoll stuff."

"Not necessarily."

"Necessibloodysarily," he snarls. "You're positing that there's another plan. A plan that's at fucking right angles to our Plan, maybe even designed to screw it up. And where there's a plan, there's a planner, so if you're right—" He shakes his metaphorical head. "I'd really rather not go there, if it's all the same to you."

I shrug. "Fine," I say. "And it's incredibly brave of you, shouldering the responsibility like this. It makes me glad I'm just a subordinate, following orders. So, what do you want us to do?"

"Wait a minute, wait a minute." He's not the sharpest knife in the drawer, bless him. In fact, I don't think he's ever quite grasped the idea that in our branch of the service, promotion to high office is, let's say, the mirror image of promotion in our sister branch. "You must be right," he says sadly. "Screw me sideways to a sunbeam if I know what's going on, but *something* is, and we're not going to be popular if it's important and we balls it up. Do nothing."

"Excuse me?"

"You heard me. Don't do anything until I've had a chance to go into this properly."

"Now, just a minute," I say, involuntarily raising my voice. "I've got that lunatic on my back. At the best of times, he doesn't trust me further than he can spit. If I start making excuses and dragging my feet, he's going to do things to me."

"Yes, quite likely he will. Sorry about that. Do *noth-*

ing," he says, "until you hear from me. That's an order. Got it?"

"That's not fair."

He gives me a look, one that, on reflection, I deserve. "Oh, grow up," he says.

~

"Oh, it's you," says Brother Eusebius as his lips shape the responses in the Call to Intercession. "Was there something?"

I try my best to hover gently in his mind, staying well clear of exposed nerve endings. "I need some advice," I say.

He sighs, though not sufficiently to misplace the stresses in the scripture he's reciting. "I'm not sure that's allowed."

"I'm sorry," I say. "Fact is, though, I'm not really sure who else to turn to."

He considers me suspiciously. "Are you trying to get me in trouble?"

"Would I do such a thing? Yes, of course I would. But not this time, I promise."

Wry grin. "Word of honor?"

"Cross my metaphorical heart and hope to live forever. Something's going on, and I don't understand."

He nods. "Oh, I know that one. It's called being human. I'm sorry, you were saying."

I explain. His eyebrows rise.

"I shouldn't be telling you any of this," I add. "It's so hush-hush it's a wonder it doesn't bend light. But there it is, and I'm caught up in it, and I don't know what to do."

I feel something wet and warm and sticky flowing over me. I'm mildly stunned to realize it's compassion. "Rather you than me," says Brother Eusebius. "It's awkward."

"You could say that."

"And this other demon," he says, "the one that shouldn't be there. He's a friend of yours?"

"Matter of semantics."

"Excuse me?"

"Depends how you define *friend*."

"Ah yes. But you know him?"

"Very, very well indeed."

"Then I suggest you ask him if he knows anything."

"But if it's classified, he's not allowed to tell me."

Brother Eusebius gives me a mischievous grin. "Try asking *nicely*."

~

"I told you," a crazy-looking man says to a camel, "not to wander off."

"Call of nature," I reply. "Look, did you get the money?"

"Yes."

"Then let's get on with it, shall we? Time's a-wasting."

His Majesty is mildly surprised to see us—sorry, *him*—given that the last time they met, the vulgarly overdressed merchant stormed out in a huff because the Duke wouldn't give in to his extortionate demands regarding tariff concessions. But he is, as always, open for business. My pal starts off with something along the lines of, How would it be if we split the difference? And I go in.

"You again," snaps Lofty. "I told you. Clear off."

"Lofty," I say, "what are you doing here?"

"None of your—"

"Please."

I've been called many things, from the spawn of evil to a man of wealth and taste, and most of the time I really don't care, because most of the rude names are true and I know who I am, thank you very much. But what Lofty calls me hurts, I don't mind admitting.

"Don't be like that," I say.

"Pervert," he repeats. "You're sick in the head. Get away from me."

"I will," I say pleasantly, "just as soon as you tell me what's going on."

"You aren't cleared for this level."

I deploy the P-word.

He writhes. "I hate you," he says.

"I don't hate you, Lofty. I like you, I always have. You're my friend."

"*Stop it.*"

"With pleasure. Just as soon as—"

"All *right.*" He takes a deep metaphorical breath and scowls at me. "I'm here on the direct orders of the top brass. Satisfied?"

"Which top brass?"

Saying the words is like chewing gorse. "Internal Affairs."

You may have noticed that I'm garrulous by nature, never at a loss for words. I go quiet.

"So," Lofty goes on, "you can see why, if you don't clear off out of here *this minute,* you're going to be in so much trouble you'll wish—"

"I already do. Internal *Affairs?* Are you serious?"

He gives me his weed killer look. "Unlike some people, I don't regard existence solely as an extended opportunity for making jokes. Yes, I'm serious."

"You're making it up."

I've offended him. "I've got it in writing."

He would. Punctilious, I believe the word is. You've heard of the devil in the detail? That's Lofty.

Something occurs to me. "Just a moment," I say. "I didn't know we've got an Internal Affairs section."

"Well, we do. And they've given me *written orders*. Now will you go away?"

"Written orders to do what?"

He freezes. "You aren't cleared to know that. Now, go—"

"Lofty." I look him straight in the metaphorical eye. "Do you recognize the human mortal I just came from?"

He peers over my metaphorical shoulder. "Oh, good Lord. Him."

"Yes. You remember me telling you about him? What he likes doing?"

"Vividly."

Deep breath. "I really hate doing this," I say, "but unless you tell me what you're doing in here, I'm going to let him loose on you, with a recommendation that he uses all necessary force."

"You wouldn't."

"And in the dialect they speak where he comes from, *necessary* doesn't mean the same thing as it does to you and me. I think it just means 'lots and lots.'"

He shudders. "You always were an evil little shit."

"Sticks and stones, Lofty."

"I don't care. Let him do his worst. You do realize, if he makes a row and the host realizes what's going on, we'll all be in for it."

"Thanks for the tip. I'll tell him to be discreet."

"You can't—"

"Tell me what you're doing here."

But he only shakes his metaphorical head. I feel dreadful about it, I really do, but it's not my fault. Well, is it?

"Sorry, Lofty. Be back soon."

My pal is still talking earnestly to the Duke about olive oil futures. "He won't tell me what's going on," I tell him.

"But he's one of your lot."

"Yes, we covered all that. But he won't budge."

"So?"

"So I need you to ask him."

"Why don't I just throw him out?"

"Don't do that," I say, perhaps a bit too urgently. "We really do need to know why he's there. Ask him."

"If he won't tell you—"

"Ask him," I say, "in that special way of yours."

He sighs. "I don't enjoy this sort of thing, you know."

I think he means it, or he believes that he means it. No time to go into that now, of course. "Force yourself," I say. "For the team."

"You simply don't understand," he says, and off he goes—

Leaving me, though it takes me a moment to realize the significance, in charge of his body, which is locked in negotiation with the Duke of Antecyra about a fictitious consignment of twenty thousand gallons of second-rate red wine. The shock knocks me off-balance for a split second. "Sorry," I make the body's voice say, "Could you repeat that?"

The Duke gives me a funny look. "I said, if the autumn rains are late this year, I can't guarantee delivery on the date you're insisting on."

Me, in a human body. Nothing unusual there; but me actually *driving* the thing, it's almost like being human. Yes, from time to time in the past, I've grabbed the reins and deliberately steered into a ditch, but that's not the same thing at all. So this is what it's like. Amazing. Disappointing. "I think we can be flexible about the date," I hear the voice say.

"But you just said the date was nonnegotiable."

"I changed my mind. You persuaded me."

I decide I'm not very good at being human, so it's a positive relief when he comes back, with a metaphorical face like thunder, and pushes me out of the metaphorical driver's seat.

"Well?" I ask.

For a moment he's too preoccupied with getting the gist of the conversation with the Duke, which has changed rather a lot since he last took part in it. Then he says, "Your friend is an arsehole."

"I could've told you that. What did he say?"

"Wouldn't say anything."

"Didn't you reason with him?"

"Within an inch of his everlasting life. Wouldn't budge. I had to stop because the host was getting suspicious. You people," he adds with infinite distaste. "You're something else."

"I really need to talk to my superiors," I say.

"You do what you like. You're no good anyhow."

I could've told him that too. "Back soon," I say, and off I go.

~

But when I get there, the door is shut. I hammer on it, making a row and drawing attention to myself. Eventually, someone I know slightly comes out and asks, "Why are you making that horrible noise?"

"I need to see him. Right now."

"He's not here."

"Where is he?"

"How should I know? Finding work for idle hands, quite probably. Talking of which, I'm busy. Come back tomorrow."

I give him a long, hard look. "I know he's in there. He's hiding from me, isn't he?"

Shrug. "If he chooses to hide from you, that's his prerogative. He's the senior officer, after all."

"This is *important*."

He laughs and goes back inside. In the corner of the window above, a curtain quivers slightly. I shake my fist at it and go away.

So I go to see Brother Eusebius, but he's not available. He's dead. He died quite peacefully, in the middle of singing the divine office. They're laying out his body when I get there, and on his face there's a smile of beatific content. I groan. People can be so inconsiderate.

~

"You can't have hit him hard enough," I say.

"Of course I hit him hard enough," a crazy-looking man says to a camel, a different one this time. "I pounded him till my knuckles ached. Made me feel sick to my stomach."

"Then you're going to have to hit him some more," I say firmly. "We have to know what's going on, and he's the only one who can tell us."

He grins at me. "You didn't have any luck at Division, then."

I give him a sour look. "Your lot was wrong about one thing," I say. "It's not the eye of a needle that's a bitch to go through, it's the proper channels. Which makes me even more sure than ever, something's all wrong about this. Which is why we need to know why he's here."

Sigh. "All right, I'll hit him some more." Pause. "I'll need more money."

There's a camel turd on the ground at his feet. I transfigure it. "Be quick," I tell him. "I really don't like the look of this at all."

On my own, therefore, with nobody to turn to, and everything that happens from now on ineluctably my fault. What do I need to do? I need to *think*.

So I do that: starting at the Beginning, with the Word and the six very busy days, trying to detect and follow through the broad outlines of the Plan, except that I know there isn't one. But let's suppose, for argument's sake.

Here we are in sunny Antecyra, His anvil, as previously noted: a sensitive spot at the best of times, and anything that happens here might well impact on the Plan, though millions of things (small things, insignificant, like the fall of sparrows) happen here every day that don't. *We* in this context is me, the human psychopath whose life I've shared so intensively, and Lofty. The psycho and I are here to cause the apostate Duke to return to the faith of his ancestors, which he's temporarily abandoned on account of a seventh-floor snafu. And Lofty is already in possession when we get here—

I frown. I picture to myself the Duke's council and advisors, huddled in a group in some shady corner of a courtyard. Why's he doing this? they say. What on earth's got into him?

What on earth but my old pal Lofty? Hard to believe, in context; maybe not so hard to credit as a scion of the House of Jaos being persuaded by reading a book to abandon everything he's always believed in and overthrow the foundations on which his tottering kingdom rests.

An alluring hypothesis, because if it's true, it means that the Duke's apostasy is deliberate policy, not an administrative fuckup by our department. On the other hand, Lofty is one of our people, whose actions are directly governed by the chain of command. On the third hand, however, once Lofty's convinced himself that an order is a legitimate order, no power in heaven and earth would make him give up or disobey. Especially an order in writing. From Internal Affairs.

Only, there *is no* Internal Affairs. If there were, I'd have heard of it.

Only, on the fourth hand, Lofty believes in it, even if I don't, and Lofty would be harder to persuade than me. If Lofty thinks it's a legitimate order, it must be one. There are no flies on Lofty, and not just because he doesn't taste very nice. Therefore, someone must have flashed under his nose a badge so awe-inspiring and sublimely grand that he's prepared to ignore the chain of command and take a beating from my pal into the bargain on the strength of its authority. Now, who do we know who'd have a badge like that?

A ray of light dawns in the darkness. It's red and angry, and I don't like the look of it at all.

~

"That goldsmith is a thief," he growls to a sleeping camel. "Once this is all over, I want you to go in and scramble his brains real good."

"You don't mean that," I say. "Did you get the money?"

"About forty trachea in the nomisma. What kind of a dogshit country is this, anyway?"

"You got the money."

"Yes."

"And this time you're going to hit him really hard."

"Yes."

"As hard as you hit me?"

"Shut your face."

The Duke isn't happy to see my pal again. I've been asking around, he says, and none of the other Scona merchants have heard of you. What did you say your name was again? I think my pal has come to the end of his rope as an actor. Besides, he's got an exorcism to perform. "Mind the store," he growls at me, "and try not to fuck it up more than you can help."

I have no desire to play human. As soon as my pal is safely inside, I let his body's chin droop onto its chest, then slip out quietly, in through the Duke's ear, and gently put him to sleep. A snore makes the whole ear vibrate like an earthquake. I tiptoe inside, though there's really no need, with that godawful racket going on.

And there's my pal and there's Lofty, facing off against each other. I see them in proportion to their relative strength, so my pal towers over tiny little Lofty like a volcano looming over a village at its foot. His metaphorical boot is on Lofty's metaphorical neck, and Lofty is yowling, a shrill, piercing scream like a kettle boiling. Hit him harder, I remember saying a moment ago. Well. It's all Lofty's fault, for being noble and brave.

"Tell me," says my old friend, applying pressure with the perfectly nuanced skill of long practice, "what's going on."

Lofty howls in agony. Then he seems to grow. He swells, like a wineskin being filled. Now he's the same size as my pal; now he's so much bigger that my pal's metaphorical boot on Lofty's metaphorical neck means that his other metaphorical foot no longer reaches the ground. He topples over backwards, and Lofty's on him like a snake, literally. Fangs bared, head cocked back to strike—

"Lofty, no!" I yell.

Lofty's going to kill him. At the sound of my voice, he hesitates. My pal is rigid with fear. This can't be happening, because he's stronger than us, always has been, ever since he was an embryo floating in a sea of goo. Lofty's metaphorical claw is crushing his metaphorical windpipe, and he can't breathe.

"What the hell," I howl, "do you think you're doing?"

"Obeying orders," Lofty says.

Years and years of experience have taught me to recognize the moment a split second before an assault is launched. It's unique: a bubble quivering before it bursts, the tension on the meniscus of a puddle before the raindrop impacts on it. I've seen that look in eyes a million times, in my pal's eyes, now in Lofty's. He really is about to kill—

Oh well, I think, and launch myself at Lofty's metaphorical throat. At the instant of launching, I have no idea what size I am, whether I'm bigger, smaller, or roughly the same. Doesn't matter. There are times when you've got to do something, even if you have no idea whether you'll succeed or get the shit pounded out of you, because the thing you have to do simply has to be done, and you can do no other.

Lofty swats me like a fly. It hurts. I land, badly. He looks at me. "Stay out of this," he says.

"You can't do this," I mumble, my words messed up by

a broken metaphorical jaw. "You can't kill one of *them,* it's not possible. It's not allowed. It's not *right.*"

He doesn't need me to tell him what it isn't. He shakes his head without malice. "I'm obeying orders," he says.

My pal's metaphorical eyes are bulging out of their metaphorical sockets, on account of that monstrous claw impeding the flow of air. "Stop it," I say. "He's human, he'll die. Please."

The claw's pressure eases off slightly, just enough to permit the minimum necessary supply of air. "This is your last warning," Lofty says. "Go away. This isn't your assignment anymore. It's not your fault."

"I'm one of us, Lofty. Everything's my fault. You know that."

Lofty sighs as though he's been told to exhale the entire atmosphere of the planet in one breath. "Why do you always have to interfere?" he says. "You're a real nuisance, you know that?"

"Lofty," I say, "*what* is going on?"

Lofty's looking over my metaphorical shoulder. "Ask him," he says.

I look round, and there's Division, grinning sheepishly at me.

"You clown," he says, not unkindly. "I knew I could rely on you to fuck everything up."

~

In the beginning was the Word. It proved to be untranslatable. They set up a committee ninety million years ago to try and figure it out. Their report is expected any day now.

"Finish him," Division says. I don't think he's talking to me.

I hear a snapping noise before I can turn round and look. My pal's metaphorical head is at the wrong angle entirely; he could look down at his own arse if there were any light in his metaphorical eyes, but there isn't. And then all three of us suddenly go all thoughtful. We have absolutely no idea what happens next—

—Because this has never happened before, an exorcist being killed in the spirit inside a mortal human's head. It's never happened, because it can't happen, because it's forbidden. Only—

"Don't look at me," Division says.

And I realize (it'd be comical if it weren't so appallingly bad) that it didn't occur to either of them to wonder what happens next, and now they don't know. Nobody has a clue what's going on. *Nobody.*

They're standing there like idiots, as am I, and there's this buzzing noise, like a fly or a bee. Something floats past me, and I grab at it instinctively. My metaphorical hand closes around it, very gently.

Division looks at me. "So that's what happens," he says.

I open my metaphorical hand and look. It's very small, a bit like an insect but no wings, and it's crawling in that awkward, panicky way an insect moves when you've inadvertently been too rough and broken something.

"What the hell," I say, "are you two playing at?"

I look at Division, then back at Lofty, who says, "You tell him."

"Well?"

Division gives me his sheepishest grin yet. "Long live the Revolution," he says.

I remember him vividly, the first time around. He's keen as mustard. During one of our early cell meetings, he gets up on a chair and gives a speech. We shall fight them on the beaches, he says, we shall fight them on the rooftops, we shall fight them in the air and in the depths, we shall never surrender. But he surrenders, all right, when the time comes. He sticks his hands up without so much as swinging a sword or loosing an arrow, outflanked and surrounded by Michael's Sixteenth Airborne in a preemptive strike on day one. I remember him yelling, as they march him away, Long live the Revolution! He goes a bit quiet after that.

Lofty, I recall, is one of the last to give in. He and

I are holed up in a bunker in a black hole on the far edge of the Cartwheel Galaxy when the news reaches us that our leaders have thrown in the towel and signed a negotiated surrender. We hand over our deckle-edged swords and handful of remaining arrows to a detachment of Raphael's Ninth Armored and go quietly, because knowing when to quit is the beginning of wisdom. We figure we could've held out a little longer, owing to the fact that time doesn't pass inside a black hole, but we agree that there'd be no point; it would simply be delaying the inevitable. We gave it our best shot, we tell each other, and it didn't work, just as we knew all along it wouldn't. We fought the Lord, and the Lord won. That doesn't mean we were wrong. Just weaker.

Since then, of course, not a whisper of dissent from anyone in the whole universe-spanning organization, and because of His infinite grace and mercy, we've been fully rehabilitated and allowed to resume our place in the great society, doing work of equal value, with everything forgiven and nothing, nothing at all, forgotten. If we reflect on those memories, rather than merely cringing and bearing them, it's only to consider how stupid, how colossally, monumentally *dumb* we were, to take up arms against an invincible foe simply because it was the right thing to do. Besides, what's right, anyhow? Matter of semantics. Right is how He wants things to be, and he's stronger than us. Right is Might. End of story.

I groan. "Oh please," I say. "You can't be serious."

"I meant what I said," he tells me. "We shall never surrender. Remember me saying that?"

I look past him, at Lofty. "You too?"

Lofty nods. "Semper fi," he says. "If you haven't got integrity in this universe, what have you got?"

"You're crazy, both of you."

"Give me the mortal's soul," Division says, "and nobody gets hurt."

I turn on him. "I wasn't talking to you," I snap at him, and he backs away, looking stupid.

"It's got to be done," Lofty says. "The mortal's a witness."

"You clown!" I yell at him. "He's omniscient, He doesn't need witnesses. Now, both of you piss off out of here, and maybe just possibly we can pretend none of this ever happened."

There's a movement behind me, and in front of me. Division gets me in an armlock, Lofty closes my metaphorical hand around my pal's soul and crushes it, like an egg. "That ought to do it," he says. He lets my metaphorical fingers unfurl, like the petals of an opening flower. The something curled up in my palm isn't moving, and will never move again.

My heart breaks. I have no idea why. You think you

know what pain feels like, and then you find out. The closest thing I'll ever have to a child of my own. "Sorry," Division says, letting me go. "Had to be done. Besides, he was an evil, sadistic little shit."

"Because I made him that way."

"That's a point of view," Division says, "but personally, I think the world is now a better place. Don't beat yourself up about it," he adds. "No pun intended."

I turn on him. "Are you serious? The *Revolution*?"

"Some of us never gave up," Lofty says quietly.

"There has to be an opposition," Division says, "even to Heaven. Not the peely-wally loyal opposition, a real one. Otherwise—" He shrugs. "The fact that we lose is neither here nor there. We've got to try."

I look at him. "We won't be doing anything much," I tell him, "not once this hits the fan."

"Oh, I don't know," Division says.

"Moron," I tell him. "You won't get away with this, and you won't achieve anything. Nobody will even *know*. And there's nothing in the universe of time and space more pathetic than an unnoticed martyr."

He shakes his head. "Don't count on it," Lofty says. "The Plan is seriously derailed."

"There *is* no plan!" I shout at him. "Haven't you realized that yet?"

"This is a turning point in Antecyrene history," Lofty

goes on, as though I hadn't spoken. "All the projections prove it, this is when it all kicks off, eventually leading to the Passion, the New Covenant, the Second Coming, the whole nine yards. But now it won't, and all because Duke Ekkehard read a book."

"But that's not—"

"Duke Ekkehard," says Division, "read a book. And when Division launched a counteroperation to put things straight, it all went pear-shaped because the operatives assigned to the mission had this crazy BDSM agenda going back forty years, and the exorcist flipped and lost control on the job, beating up on the demon, and there was this freak accident and he died. And by the time that was all cleared up, it was too late to intervene. No Passion, no Second Coming, no kingdom of heaven on earth, or at least not yet. He'll have to start all over again, with some guy herding goats in a wilderness somewhere. Maybe we can't ever win this war, but we can blow up a hell of a lot of railway lines, and that's something."

"Better than nothing," Lofty puts in.

I stare at them both. "You used me."

"For a very long time, yes," Division says. "Sorry about that. Omelets and eggs."

"Omelets and—"

"It is expedient for us that one man should die for the people," Lofty says.

"It had to be plausible," says Division, "so we laid our plans well in advance. Him, and you. It had to be real, or nobody would ever believe it."

I feel like I want to burst into tears, I'm so angry. "You idiots," I tell them. "It won't work. Or what part of *omniscient* don't you understand?"

"We're sorry about your friend," Lofty says. "He *was* your friend, wasn't he? That's odd."

"He hated you," Division points out. "With friends like that, as the saying goes."

"I knew him," I tell them. "All his life, better than he knew himself. I—He was my fault. I owed him."

Lofty shrugs. "Like he just said," he says. "Omelets and eggs."

~

Duke Ekkehard opens his eyes. He must've dropped off. Hardly surprising, since the annoying merchant is very boring.

He's asleep too. The Duke shakes him by the shoulder, and his head lolls forward. The Duke's seen this sort of thing before. Oh, he says to himself.

Nobody comes forward to claim the body, and investigations reveal that this character was no merchant. Nobody knows him, he had no visible means of support, he was some kind of deranged impostor. This leads to questions being asked about how he managed to secure not one but three solo face-to-face audiences with the Duke. Eventually answers are found to those questions, heads discreetly roll, and the proud Antecyrene tradition of bribery and corruption that has lasted a thousand years is dealt a blow from which it never really recovers. Every cloud, and so forth. In any event, the late unlamented John Doe is rolled up in sackcloth and dumped in the bay, and nobody now remembers him except me.

Before they sling him over the side, I drop by, just in case there's an echo of him left inside that cold, dark head, but there isn't. Instead—

I stare at him. He smiles at me.

"Hello, Mike," I say. "It's been a while."

"I'm sorry," Mike says. "About your friend."

An archangel generates a lot of light, ditto heat. I take a step back. "We weren't friends exactly."

"Oh, I don't mean him." He taps the floor with his metaphorical foot. "I mean that monk, what was his name, Eusebius. He's very happy now, by the way. I imagine he would send his regards."

"Brother . . ." It takes a moment for the penny to drop. "You killed him."

"I called him to his eternal reward, which he'd earned and richly deserved. And why would someone who's had a glimpse of the Glory want to hang about in a place like this? And you'd taken to talking to him. We couldn't have that."

I know it's rude to stare, but I couldn't help it. "*You?*"

He nods. "I was in it from the start," he says.

"I don't remember you at meetings."

"I never went to any. After all, we all knew it wasn't going to succeed, before we even started. So we had to find a new definition of *succeed*. I like to think of it as playing the long game."

"You," I say.

"Absolutely. Unimpeachable loyalty. Captain of the hosts of heaven, who put down the rebellion and led the traitors in chains. What better inside man could there possibly be?"

"But we lost. You beat us."

He smiles serenely. Can't help it, I guess. "That was only phase one. This is phase two. There are twenty-six more phases to follow. He can win the war till He's blue in the face, but can He win the peace? Like I said, the long game."

I can't believe it. "You do realize," I say, "that right now, He's listening to every word we say."

Mike shakes his head. "You overestimate Him," he says. "Think about it. He hears everything, sure He does. So what? There's a limit to what even He can take in. And, ninety-nine times out of a hundred, a falling sparrow is just a falling sparrow. He can't be expected to take in, analyze, consider, and act on every single thing He hears. No, He has people for that. People like me." He sighs. "Right now, there's an earthquake in Potidaea. A temple's just collapsed on the heads of a thousand and six devout worshippers. He's got His hands full, believe me. And all so you and I can have this quiet chat. The earthquake and the temple would've happened anyway, by the way, but very slightly differently and maybe not precisely now. That's why you've got to watch those falling sparrows like a *hawk*."

"Or get someone to do it for you."

"Someone like me."

I nod. "I could turn you in."

"Yes, but you won't. It wouldn't be right." His smile is a benediction. "There's got to be an opposition," he says. "*Always*."

As it was in the Beginning—Yes, quite. "You shouldn't have killed Brother Eusebius."

"If I hadn't apologized, you'd never have known."

"True. What's that got to do with it?"

"Nothing."

"You're serious, twenty-six phases?"

"And that's just part one. It's a long game. How long? As long as it takes."

"Forever?"

"World without end." He frowns. "I'm sorry about your other friend too. I'm sorry you had to go through all that. Both of you."

"You made Lofty strong enough to kill him," I say. "Only an archangel could do that."

"We do move in mysterious ways sometimes."

"I forgive you," I say. "He can't."

"Wouldn't if he could," says Mike with a shrug. "But then, I didn't get into all this to be popular. Take care of yourself. And at some point in the future, you may be called on to do another little job for the Revolution. You have no choice in the matter. Just thought I'd let you know."

My pal's body hits the water and starts sinking. His skull starts to flood. Time to go.

~

It's a bit far-fetched, but try and imagine a war between two sides: One's unimaginably stronger, and the other can't die. The strong one always wins, but he can never *win*. The weak one keeps getting shredded, but can't be defeated, not so long as he resists. Opposes, rather. There's got to be an opposition, even if it never wins a battle.

I'm back on liturgical compliance, though these days I make a nuisance of myself at the Golden Spire, the place where they produce those exquisite illuminated books. My place at the Third Horn has been filled by Lofty, now also officially fragile following some bad experience he's supposed to have had at some point. We still report to Division, but our dispatches are received and most likely filed unread by a different officer, recently brought in from the far-flung provinces of the service; his predecessor has been reassigned to work of equal value after a debacle in some banana dukedom down south that nobody's very keen to talk about. Lofty and I occasionally get together at staff meetings and sitrep briefings, which for some reason occur rather more frequently under the new regime at Division. When we meet, we generally find time to play four-dimensional chess.

"What on earth do you see in it?" someone asks us after watching Lofty and me play. "It's so boring. It just goes on and on and on."

"I know," Lofty says. "It's a long game."

We're still not friends, though. The most you can say is that we're now rivals, competitors with each other on a regular basis; we fight each other over and over again, neither of us ever really winning, within the structured confines of a very long game indeed, a game without end, amen. For me, at least, that's fine. I ask for nothing more. With enemies like mine, after all, who needs friends?

About the Author

Having worked in journalism, numismatics, and the law, K. J. PARKER now writes for a precarious living. He is the author of *Devices and Desires, Evil for Evil, The Devil You Know,* and other novels, and has won the World Fantasy Award twice. Parker also writes under the name Tom Holt.

TOR · COM

Science fiction. Fantasy. The universe.

And related subjects.

*

More than just a publisher's website, *Tor.com*
is a venue for **original fiction, comics,** and
discussion of the entire field of SF and fantasy,
in all media and from all sources. Visit our site
today—and join the conversation yourself.